DEMIGODS

by

J. Giambrone

Published by Indies United Publishing House, LLC

© *Copyright 2019, Joe Giambrone*

Paperback Edition

ISBN: 978-1-64456-049-5 / 1-64456-049-6

Based on the motion picture screenplay 'DEMIGODS'

Copyrighted 2010, Joe Giambrone

Library of Congress Control Number 1-489905421

Indies United Publishing House LLC.

P.O. Box 3071

Quincy, Illinois 62305-3071

http://www.indiesunited.net/

3

For the unknown heroes who gave all
because it was the right thing to do.

DEMIGODS

PROLOGUE

He spun in the fog of a daze, his muscles stiff from atrophy, and he felt uncoordinated, but much more. Body ill in some vague, distant way, he had become something inhuman. Hearing things beyond the audible spectrum, radio waves, cell-phone data, these spectra squeaked past low in the distance. Another frequency range churned inside his guts, a darker spectrum. His mind encapsulated in the black liquid, he found himself engulfed by the dark-matter catalyst. Crossing over between the two universes, the other side beckoned him with siren calls.

"What does he mean? Transmogrify?"

His mind overwhelmed to the point of madness, his senses flared. As he scrutinized his hands, he recalled that his name was Steve something. His gaze fell upon what remained of that scientist, a stiff, charred lump in the corner of the floor.

The house's structure had been damaged by some cataclysmic event. Medical machines had crashed across the floor. One wire was still tethered into his arm. The line snaked back toward a soft blue glow on the floor.

In his mad delirium, Steve tore out the catheter and stepped on to inspect the smoky hallway. Tiptoeing down a wooden staircase and toward the source of the fire, he squinted to peer across the concrete cellar. A final stair below him had been mangled from some blast event, and it cracked in half.

"Dammit!"

He fell face forward toward the dirty cement floor. Pressing his hands out to catch himself, his body hovered a foot above the ground. When he reclaimed his bearings, he looked over at the devastation through the dark, caustic smoke.

The force of his will propelled him up and away

from the floor. He righted himself. Feet crunched down onto some debris beneath.

His fingers pinched himself, but his nerves had all numbed. Steve felt nothing, no temperature. He inhaled, but it seemed unnecessary. A darkened veil had settled before his eyes contorting the light and the colors. A darker reality tingled inside of his body. It coursed and throbbed throughout him with energy to spare. Dark matter forces coiled onto his fibers with each cell ensnared. That second engine within him roared of its own accord. If it expanded he might explode in a gory mist.

The basement laboratory had cratered down at the point of some explosion. The cluttered expanse was littered with melted glass and contorted steel racks. Steve saw a pulsing yellow glow beneath the wreckage. Minuscule particles crackled randomly like sparklers unleashed, but it was like nothing he'd seen before. His eyes registered colors beyond the normal human range.

It dawned on him that he could only see these things with his newfound dark vision.

"Is that radiation?"

Steve gawked at the sparklers, and then he quickly turned and got the hell out of there. Upstairs, the large multi-story house stood intact. The air still smoky, but the building structure seemed salvageable.

Steve attempted a search through his memories to recall who he was and where he'd come from. Inside his smothered mind remained a towering, impenetrable black wall.

"Why am I here?"

His feet stepped up to the home's front door. When he yanked it open, the blinding cyan glare frightened him at first. His eyes rapidly adjusted. His attention locked onto a pile of old newspapers left laying on the front porch. He scurried out and pulled them into his chest. Escaping the oddly colored sun pulsing above, streaked in browns and turquoise, Steve hid from the light back inside the hazy living room.

As he pieced together his location, he forced his eyes shut again, diving down in a quest to understand his former life. Try as he might to break out of the surrounding blackness, his brain had been sucked into a kind of black hole.

Steve lay that night upstairs in the scientist's bed.

Imagining a plan of action, he considered to simply take over the residence and clean it up, bury the body. He had a positive feeling about working with tools and repairing things, and he wanted to be useful.

At long last he fell asleep.

That face, the beautiful girl, he knew her. He loved her purely. But she strolled away with a little boy, a kid. It was Cathy and Michael. They turned back and waved him on to invite him along.

Steve wanted to follow and to stay with them, but his legs went uselessly limp. Crawling hand over hand, he pulled himself along the mushy ground to catch up. They refused to slow down, the woman and the boy, despite his calling.

Soon he was alone and abandoned shivering in the dark. Up in the swirling black sky the dropping rain became shards of ice and hail. The barrage sliced into his arms as he shielded his eyes in a snow-blind assault.

Jolting out of the scientist's bed, Steve flew up. His head crashed through the ceiling tiles. His skull splintered the two-by-four beam above the bedroom and lodged in between the cracked wooden pieces.

"What the hell!"

As he extricated his head from the building with

care, he peered down onto the bedroom below through the dim dust. His body floated effortlessly on the air. Gentle unseen currents bobbed like he could swim through the atmosphere.

He was a man, but he floated on the air.

"What the hell am I?"

ONE

D'Andre heard the heavy nurse Shondra right outside his hospital room, "Dammit not agai-in!"

All the ceiling lights flickered in a brown-out. His TV jolted and turned itself off. The room turned to grey. He sat back against a pillow watching the dirty sunlight splash in through his sixth-floor window. Traffic noises returned. With no way of knowing how long it might last, he considered whether he should get out of bed today and see what was going on out there in the ward.

The electricity blasted again back to normal, and D'Andre heard the celebrations of the other kids out on the main floor. Dozens returned to their screens and restarted their video games.

Hospital life returned to normal. The facility sat in the heart of the Bronx, and its walls needed re-painting. Once the images returned to his TV set, D'Andre relaxed his bald head back onto his pillow. He felt too tired to fuss or to change the channel. It was more news, so much news. It never stopped.

He had his own problems.

After his hair fell out, his Grandpops told him, "Look over there for a second, boy. Go on. What's that?"

Grandpops was huge, his deep voice commanding.

D'Andre turned. "What? There's nuthin' there."

"Hm. Hm, hm, hm, hmmm."

"What's wrong?" D'Andre turned back, confused.

"Boy," said Grandpops, "the back a your head looks like a *Milk Dud* or a *Whoppers*. That's the one. Better watch out them nurses out there gonna eat you up."

"Oh, Grandpops."

"No. That big, that heavy-set mama nurse. I'm tellin' ya. Keep one eye open. She definitely got an appetite, that one."

"Oh you trippin."

The two laughed.

"Ah, D'Andre. What am I gonna do? I gotta get to work."

"It's all right. I like it here."

Grandpops worked six days in a factory, and the seventh didn't always work out. D'Andre lay alone for long stretches with just his TV to fill his thoughts. He was ten now but not confident he would see eleven.

"Oww," he felt his belly. "Damn."

Pudgy nurse Shondra poked her head into his room. "You all right there, little man?"

"It just achy."

"Is it like sharp?"

He shook his head.

Nurse Shondra came in to inspect. Her fat fingers gently prodded around his belly. "That hurt?"

D'Andre shrugged, and he looked off wincing.

"A-ight. I'm gonna tell the doctor stop by. Okay?"

He nodded, and nurse Shondra strolled out.

On the wall, the TV news played.

Nurse Shondra popped her head back in. "Doc'll be by this afternoon. Okay? How you holdin' up D'Andre?"

"I'm tired, Miss Shondra."

"Well you *know* what's comin' on at noon time?"

"Yeah. Maybe I'll just watch in here."

"Well, everybody's gonna gather round in the rec room, like they always do."

D'Andre shrugged, and he closed his eyes.

Nurse Shondra stepped closer with a hushed voice. "I'll tell you what I gots for you."

"Huh?"

"Just came in this mornin'. An electro-powered, motorized, turbo-charged wheelchair. Ain't nobody tried it out yet. It's brand new."

D'Andre perked up. "Oh yeah?"

"I'll come back about a quarter til. Now you be ready."

He nodded and watched her prance back out of his room. The steel IV needle poking in between his knuckles agitated him, and he wanted to rip it out again, but something caught his attention above. A quickly assembled news report from Bolivia of all places. The TV headline said, *"Supernaturals Involved?"*

D'Andre jerked to attention.

Crowds of brown peasant villagers shouted and marched with signs in some protest. The news asked, *Were Supernaturals Sighted?*

A crying Bolivian woman lay down a lifeless baby onto a colorful blanket. "Los Diablos!"

More women gathered around the still baby, forming the sign of the cross repeatedly and praying with Rosary beads.

"Bebé es Muerto!" Another village woman screamed at the news cameras.

The broadcast cut short. The network played a commercial.

D'Andre waited through the commercial break for an explanation about the Supernatural sighting, but it never came. Sports reports told different stories. D'Andre clicked around the broadcast spectrum, hunting for news of the *Supers*, but no one else discussed it, like it never happened.

TWO

D'Andre Walker rose from his bed to gaze out of the smeary glass at the grimy urban landscape below. The big event was about to begin. He turned to his doorway, and he set out walking by himself toward the recreation room. Already the kids shouted and wrenched chairs around to sit near the big TV screen.

D'Andre trudged ahead.

Nurse Shondra called from down the hallway. "Hey D'Andre? I brought that robot chair just for you. Don't you wanna check it out?"

"Naw." He waved her off, and he claimed a seat at the back of the rec room. Everybody gathered to watch the live coverage.

The show began as usual. Out on a grassy hilltop a bunch of reporters clustered. News camera people, politicians, and in the center of it all was a little white girl named Erica Tate. The screen said she was ten, and she wore a flight suit, the kind people jumped out of airplanes in.

D'Andre watched intently, his hands quaking with anticipation.

The media circus turned skyward, and the cameras hunted across fluffy clouds. Off in the distance a little dot descended from above.

The entire hospital ward screamed out with glee. D'Andre couldn't hear the TV anymore. The kids went so wild, pointing at the screen, arguing, pushing, and pulling each other.

He ignored them to watch the landing.

Text scrolled from the news station and said that the dot was Steve "Lab Rat" Arkin, but everyone already knew that. Supernatural Steve floated easily down to the center of the hilltop and landed softly beside Erica Tate and all of the TV show people.

The kids in the rec room chattered and pointed.

Reporters described the details.

Another graphic read, *ERICA TATE, SQUAMOUS*

CELL CARCINOMA.

D'Andre tolerated the smiling spokespeople, who pushed their microphones in at Supernatural Steve, yelling silly questions.

D'Andre leaned forward, considering whether to stand up and move in closer to hear. "Come on. Let him talk!"

Assistants prepared Erica Tate to ride on Steve Arkin's back, like a tandem parachute.

Supernatural Steve gave a speech at the microphone.

"The *Wish to Dream Foundation* is a great place," he said, "and it needs your support. So write 'em a check, or click on their website. Help these kids out, okay? They need all the help they can get." He nodded, and then he relinquished the microphone to some suit.

A local politician shook Steve's hand for a photo-op with fast flashes from the cameras.

On Steve's back, Erica Tate adjusted her flight goggles, wearing ear buds. A drink holder was clipped onto Steve's shoulder.

He said, "Ready?"

The girl, Erica, said instantly, "Yeah. Let's bolt." She held her thumb up.

The rec room at the Bronx Children's Hospital exploded with cheers, as the pair flew straight up away from the crowd. Erica's helmet camera broadcast the feed. TV cameras whipped to follow Steve and Erica's quick ascent into the clouds.

The room faded away. D'Andre felt too tired to watch the rest of the show. Leaning up against the back wall of the rec room, he fell asleep.

THREE

Steven Arkin floated at a comfortable speed above the suburban landscape, in sight of the Metropolitan sprawl off to the right.

"Where to?" he asked Erica Tate, who was on his back.

They rose above the land in the whipping breeze. Over his shoulder her finger pointed.

"All right." Steve darted off north toward the fields of green on the horizon. "Is this too fast?"

"Nah! Faster!"

Arkin had his usual flight plan, and soon they arrived over a series of farms. Down to the grass, he closed fast on a herd of horses. With a tilt to his left the pair arrived beside the running animals and raced them across the pasture. Steve swerved close to fly beside a spotted white pony, which quickly fled in the opposite direction.

He heard Erica laughing.

They again flew up into the sky. At a towering waterfall, he glided to the edge of the gushing river. They were a hundred feet above the plunge.

Erica's tiny hand reached to feel the falling water.

He asked her, "You tired yet?"

"No."

He could hear the fatigue in her voice.

"All right, let's go." Rocketing to the sky again, he fired up the speed. "Hows that?"

She grabbed hold of the fabric at his shoulder, and they leveled off about ten thousand feet above the suburbs. Steve soon landed back atop that grassy hill in the park with all the reporters and his friends from the *Wish to Dream Foundation*. The organizers assisted Erica back down to earth. Her little knees wobbled.

Half a dozen microphones pushed into her face.

"Wow."

Steve knelt down, and he shook her hand. More flashes.

"Are you going to be okay, Erica?"

She nodded contently, and they seated her back into her wheelchair.

Steve stood up to announce, "I've got to get to a meeting. I'm sorry I can't stay longer."

Erica waved, and Steve flew off at high speed in another direction. He shot rapidly into orbit, where the sky turned black, much faster than regular humans could handle. Halfway across the world he descended again, buffeted by the hot friction of re-entry.

Into the dark Himalayan mountains, atop one of the world's tallest peaks, the *Council of Power* fortress remained frost-free and invisible to most. Snow and ice collected below, down the sheer rock cliff sides, but the stone palace complex was shielded from prying human eyes and rendered completely invisible. Only Supernaturals were permitted to know of its presence.

Steve remained the only human being who had ever seen the ancient fortress. It eluded eyes as well as electronic technologies. This was earth's most exclusive club, and he wasn't completely sure of his status in it.

Numerous Supernaturals arrived concurrently,

and they flew into the gaped mouth of the rock superstructure.

Steve floated down to land quietly in the courtyard at the statue of Icarus rising on eagle's wings. The inscription beneath the piece read, "Where Icarus Did Fail We Shall Prevail."

Steve strolled inside toward the extravagant creatures, where he remained an outsider, a curiosity, and barely an infant in their reality. A clique of large Supers gathered in a huddle before the entryway. They regarded Steve with suspicion.

Nukeman's molten yellow hair was unmistakable. His glowing eyes peeked back over his shoulder at Steve, and he elbowed the giant beside him, Barby the Barbarian.

Barby stood nine-feet tall, all muscle, with caveman etiquette.

Steve knew almost nothing of Nukeman, how long he had existed, or how he had come to be in this world. Whether he had always been an invisible force awaiting form and was anthropomorphized in 1945 to enter human history. Nukeman was some kind of hot energy intertwined with matter, transferring from one state to the next. Radiation unleashed through his eyes could vaporize solid rock. He was a living weapon.

The Barbarian had always been. Before men stood upright he was the largest, the fiercest, the killer instinct personified. As men longed for more strength and size, the Barbarian remained out there, the largest, the strongest, the final state of masculinity. Appearing globally in legends and folklore, Barby could humiliate the toughest brute in the entire empire and piss on his corpse for entertainment. Barby was beyond compare in Berserker ferocity and his love of violence for violence' sake. Whenever a fist clenched, the universal subconscious knowledge of Barby, out somewhere in the wild, gave the slightest moment's pause to every would-be combatant.

From thin air, a pulsing jitterbug zipped to join them. Stellar flew with incomparable speed and was difficult to track. The three of them turned belligerently in Steve's path as he attempted to skirt around them and enter the *Council* fortress, as summoned.

Nukeman called out, "You still get invites to these things, *Lab Rat?*"

Steve froze and retreated a step. "Well, I. I'm on TV often."

The giant, Barby, chortled louder than the others.

"Maybe you'll get your own sitcom! Hahaha..." Barby punched Nukeman in his biceps, sending him flying back several yards.

Stellar zipped up to Steve's face, held a menacing expression, and zapped back to the others. The three of them laughed giddily.

Barby roared the loudest. "He bother you, Lab Rat? You should kill him. Hahahaha..."

Steve knew precious little about most of the other Supernaturals of earth. Before his transformation, he held zero curiosity about the rumors and the legends. They were distant from his life and more speculation than fact. Since he'd been thrust into their midst, he found them secretive and guarded. Perhaps that was an essential component of their power.

The old myths suggested that Supernaturals had influenced human history since forever. Steve assumed they all were ancient immortals. Although, he was a newbie in their ranks, the exception to the rule.

He knew that he was distrusted.

Nukeman, Barby, and Stellar gawked back at Steve, refusing to make way for him to enter the *Great Hall*. Nukeman's demonic yellow eyes flickered like loaded weapons. The three soon lost interest in him and twisted back around to march inside of the fortress.

Nukeman paused and turned back for another go. "Hey, Lab—"

The bruisers all stopped cold, as a pale blue-white glow crept up behind them.

Out from the foyer, Miss Melt strolled through their group like a flash of lightning. She remained the singularly most enigmatic and beautiful creature on planet earth. Her hair radiated energy in colors that evolved with her changing moods. Her skin softly shimmered, and her glow left a residual trail of photons behind her as she slid past.

She strutted through the clique. "Boys."

The three retreated to the sides of the stone entrance to allow her to pass. Her sleek glowing form, in a blindingly bright dress, sauntered past the beef.

With a cat's grin, her pace never slowed as she emerged in Steve's direction. Steve faced her, alone.

Miss Melt strode right up to address him.

His eyes widened, as her white hot energy beamed out like a beacon in a cold night.

"Hello, Steven."

Nukeman, Barby, and Stellar gawked on from the shadows of the stone foyet.

Steve felt entranced and oddly weakened by Miss Melt's shifting appearance. Subliminally, he feared for his life. She was that disarming.

"Miss Melt."

"So formal!" she laughed. "Pandora."

Her glowing hand extended to shake his. As she smiled, she simultaneously whipped her head back to eyeball the three nosy onlookers. With trails of her face lingering in the air, there were momentarily two of them, and then one again.

Their gang shuffled off and disappeared into the *Great Hall.*

Miss Melt stood before Steve, and now she blocked his path inside.

When his fingers touched her radiating, feminine hand, she tingled like nothing he had ever before experienced. Her energy was not forceful so much as seductive. His brain simmered at the edge of panic, bathed in her sensuous glow.

Pandora was filled with so many types of raw power that it was beyond containing and shot out from her in every direction. The rumors were that she could melt people's minds and get them to do whatever she pleased.

"Pandora," said Steve demurely. "What can I do for you?"

She smiled back affably, her complexion taking on pink human tones. "I just think it's so noble how you entertain the little sick human children. It makes me feel something. I don't know what it is."

"Thank you." He held his feelings, careful not to ask for or reveal anything about himself.

Miss Melt's gaze danced playfully across him. "Well, don't be a stranger." She grinned.

Her transforming face hypnotized him, as it pulsed at various wavelengths. Maybe she was probing his mind.

Steve fumbled for an acceptable response, but before he could produce any words, an earth-shaking clarion call jolted the bedrock. The entire mountain bellowed with a rumbling signal that was only perceptible to creatures entangled with dark matter.

Stragglers raced in from the blackness above them to enter the palace fortress in time. Dozens of latecomers of the unseen and unimaginable variety shot past him. Steve jogged alongside Pandora into the entrance corridor, just as its massive stone doors sealed themselves behind.

Pandora turned then and her arms pinned Steve back to the rock wall of the foyer. Her touch was overwhelming, somewhere between love and electrocution. Her iridescent face filled his vision.

"I've got a secret."

Steve flattened his back against the stone. "You do?"

Miss Melt in his face, pressing him backward, and so close that her energy intermingled with his own aura. She was far too powerful, some kind of goddess from a dimension unknown.

"As if you don't," she said. Her rainbow colors flickered in orange and peach.

Steve's body vibrated, not entirely under his own control.

"Me? What would I be hiding?"

She cocked her head, so close to his mouth that he dared not move.

"Well I'll tell you mine if you tell me yours," she said.

"Honestly, I don't know what you're talking about."

She grimaced and strolled away in a frosty blue glow.

Steve comported himself, and he walked in toward the cavernous *Great Hall*. The massive room buzzed in a dark, vibrating cacophony. The clarion had streamed out to the entire Supernatural population of the earth. These *Council of Power* meetings seemed mandatory. Attendance was expected, but it was never stated outright.

Seated in rows of stone pews, the Supernatural audience included all manner of creatures, old, infirm, young, alien, animal, crystalline, dark sponges which sucked the surrounding light, and even more exotic varieties than Steve could track. Many of them faded in and out of the visible spectrum at will.

Steve sat on an empty section of a long granite bench, and he remained uncertain why the others avoided his presence. There was something about human origins that didn't sit right with Supernaturals.

His smell sense had radically altered since his crossover. He could not discern scents like a normal living creature. His perceptions were on the atomic level, with compounds, electrical currents, chemical bonds, that sort of thing. If he smelled bad, well, at least he could no longer tell.

Entering the *Great Hall* from the side of the stage,

interim President Dragomir pranced across the elevated grey stone platform at the front edge. Dragomir was half-dragon, and his leathery wings folded behind him and gently twitched. His skin was patterned in brown earth tones with traces of scales, but smooth. On his back was strapped a long silver spear.

Dragomir's black pointy fingernail tapped at a microphone, and he nodded to Miss Melt at the rear of the room.

Pandora floated to the front of the hall and up the stone staircase to join Dragomir at center stage. Everyone fixated on her glow, including Steve.

Dragomir sat back on a throne behind the podium.

As Pandora arrived to speak, her hair shifted in hue, darkening, and rearranged itself in a tight braid.

Steve gazed on her.

Pandora said, "Interim President Dragomir has recently secured numerous lucrative contracts for us with both influential human governments as well as with some of the largest corporations. I think a little applause is in order."

Dragomir feigned modesty.

The hall roared with approval. Cheers erupted

into an extended standing ovation.

Steve stood with them and clapped as the others did.

Nodding coyly, Dragomir rose to assume the podium. Pandora bowed and retreated to the side of the stage to take her own permanent stone seat.

Dragomir's voice sounded soft-spoken and well-prepared.

"In this age of technology and media inundation, let us give a mention to the human, Steven Arkin, whose face seems to appear on human television programs more often than the rest of us combined."

Dragomir pointed, and a spotlight caught Steve where he sat on the pew in the back of the gathering.

"Steven Arkin," announced Dragomir, "puts out the kind of positive Public Relations for us that money simply cannot buy. Give him a big hand, please."

The *Great Hall* applauded for Steve.

Steve stood like a curiosity at a freak show. The moment dragged on. He had never spoken with Dragomir, and this felt disquieting.

Dragomir grinned, his long face revealing oversized teeth. "Keep those kids flying high."

From across the hall, Nukeman chimed in, "You

ever drop any by mistake, *Lab Rat?* Hahaha…"

His cadre roared.

"I assure you," said Steve, "safety is my code of conduct with those fragile children. They've been through enough."

Dragomir rolled his eyes. "We love you baby. Sit down now."

Steve sat as instructed, and he gawked helplessly at Pandora at the side of the stage, peering blankly out over the Supernatural gathering. He couldn't take his eyes off of her, as he relived their frightening encounter from the way inside.

Up on the rock stage, Dragomir gazed out over the crowd of earth's Supernaturals. "The Chinese have a longstanding proverb," he said, "that crisis is merely opportunity which rides a dangerous wind…"

Pandora's glowing blue eyes caught Steve's pressing glance, and she smirked. Her eyes flashed once, like a strobe light wink.

FOUR

On the short car ride over, D'Andre Walker sat sulking in the back seat, trying to think of a way to turn the situation around.

"I don't see why I can't come too."

His mom nodded. "We already told you. It's only three days. You can come along somewhere better next time."

The car sped ahead through the New York City streets.

He jerked in anger. "I wanna go Barbados too!"

"And you will, D'Andre. Just not this time."

"Hey," his father interjected. "You best listen to

your grandpops. Don't make him mad."

"He's not gonna," said Mom.

His father turned the final corner onto Grandpops' street in Queens. "Naw I'm serious, son. Your Grandpops is old school. He don't take no shit. And he's strong. If he hits you, you ain't gettin' up."

"He's gon' be good," said Mom. "Aren't ya baby?"

"Yeah."

They arrived at the empty old house. His father unlocked the front door. "And don't mess with his stuff. Just, just, be cool. You feel me?"

"Yeah."

Mom bent down and opened up her arms. "Come here, baby." She squeezed and lifted him up off the sidewalk. "It's gonna be all right."

His Dad carried in his travel case and dropped it in the front hallway. "Hey, little man. Look at me. Some day you understand why moms and dads gotta get away once in a while. Just the two a them. Aiight? It's not a big thing for you. But it's pretty big for us. Put it here."

His Dad extended his hand for a handshake.

D'Andre grabbed it and squeezed hard.

Dad turned to leave, but paused. "Remember what I said. Don't piss him off. He just likes to drink his beer and watch his TV after a long day workin'. So let him."

D'Andre nodded. Through the living room window he watched them. Mom waved vigorously and blew him a kiss from the passenger seat. They drove off to the airport.

The old house smelled funny, like old people.

D'Andre watched cartoons for the rest of the afternoon.

The front door pushed in.

"What the hell?"

D'Andre froze.

It was Grandpops, and his gravelly voice was already in a mood.

"Hey? D'Andre? Come over here, boy."

D'Andre jolted back, and he skulked closer.

Grandpops stood massive, over six feet, all muscular, shaking his head angrily. "Hey. Don't you know to keep the door locked? What's the matter with you? Anybody coulda come up in here and done anything they want." He shook his head for emphasis.

"I, I forgot."

"You forgot. But you didn't forget to watch your cartoons, now." He shook his head again. "Priorities, boy."

"I'm sorry."

"Arright. Did ya eat?"

D'Andre shook his head no.

"Let's get some food in ya. Don't want your mother comin' sayin' I didn't feed you right. What do you like to eat?"

"I dunno."

"Hmm."

That night, lying in his dad's old single bed, D'Andre began to imagine it wasn't going to be so bad. He fell asleep.

Somebody shook hard at his arm. "Wake up. Wake up!"

"What? What?"

"There's suttom..." Grandpops was in a crazed mood, really drunk, like stumbling. "Bad... I think you need to come right now. Come out here, D'Andre."

D'Andre followed his Grandpop out to the living room where the flashing light of the TV screen lit up the old dark house. Some kind of news show played.

"I think you need to see it yourself, and make sure if it's true. Uh, oh God, I hope not." Grandpops wobbled back and forth. He'd opened up one of those old dusty whiskey bottles he kept up on his shelf.

The news story kept cutting over to some airport, and to the news studio, and back outside the airport.

"What is it?" D'Andre stepped close toward the glowing box. The blue flicker hurt his eyes less, and he could open them again.

"Just watch. Listen what they say. Listen careful." Grandpops stepped back to refill his glass full of whiskey.

The newswoman on Grandpops' TV said, "The missing flight, *Caribbean Air 322*, is now believed to have gone down just north of Bermuda."

"Wait," said D'Andre. "Which one they supposed to be on?"

Grandpops grabbed the whiskey bottle, and he guzzled down more, wiped his mouth with his shirt sleeve, didn't say nuthin'.

"Which one they supposed to be on? Grandpop?"

D'Andre started to pant uncontrollably. That's when he felt a dull pain in his belly, like he was going to curl up and fall down.

FIVE

arely perceptible radiation at 660 nanometers, the red taillight of a totaled sedan, would change the course of human evolution. The car had nosedived and crashed at the bottom of a wet ravine. The soft red glow caught the eye of a passing driver above in the storm, if only for a fraction of a second.

To his right, over the cliff, down the steep grade and into the pines, it was pure chance that LaGrange would notice the death-flicker of the automobile. Sheets of rain fought the van's steering on the slick Sierra Nevada back road, which he didn't much mind or even notice.

His van's speakers called in his own voice, as he ruminated over his latest theory, "Angular momentum of particles upon colliding with dark matter would seem in violation of the *Planck's Laws*..."

"Tel est le problème," he mumbled.

Dr. LaGrange had taken a shortcut, returning from a Los Angeles conference meeting of the *International Society of Quantum Engineers*. The society was increasingly powerful and dominated by corporate contractors who churned out quantum processors for ever-faster computing and communications. These tasks held no interest whatsoever to Claude LaGrange, who was convinced that the computers and fiber optics were plenty fast enough for our needs, and what mankind needed most was something worthy to communicate.

The curved hilltops wound above steep vertical edges. Wipers whipped, but the rushing storm smeared the darkness. In a last-moment diagonal skid, LaGrange's van nearly slipped off the road itself.

His unsure hands corrected the van's orientation, although his heart raced. The wheels below reversed slowly away from the cliff's edge to maneuver back parallel with the road.

His own audio rambled on, "This could be accounted in several manners, not least is the power spectrum density. Also hemispheric flux of the..." His finger paused the sound. He clicked the van's gear into park. Curious, he squinted at the passenger side window.

LaGrange stretched his torso long over the passenger seat and he lowered the window. Peering out at the night below, he saw the crashed car far down in the wooded abyss. It had obviously plummeted off of that narrow bit of road just as he almost had. The twinkling red glow radiated softly up through the cascading raindrops into the wider world.

Those pathetic little red lights enticed him.

Hands slid on rubber gloves and a bright yellow raincoat. LaGrange kept meticulously prepared for a variety of potential emergency situations. Out into the lashing deluge he stepped from the safety of his van to survey the steep California hillside beneath him.

That errant car, so secluded, so random. It opened a world of possibilities that could only be assessed upon closer examination.

LaGrange's rubber boots slid awkwardly on the weeds down the slick slope. Nearly falling the final distance, he scrambled through the wet plants with aplomb. Many years had passed since he'd frolicked in the rain, but the fresh joy of nature's untamed forces inspired him with *joie de vivre* and a rush of Adrenalin.

The twisted automobile wreckage lay before him, impaled on a pine tree branch, jammed straight through the windshield, a most devastating projectile.

The grotesqueness hit LaGrange.

Blood remained unwashed, splattered about the driver's corpse, a beautiful young woman, under thirty certainly. The spike had destroyed her body instantly upon impact. The horror of it all shocked him and jolted his nervous system.

LaGrange turned his head from her to the rear door, and he struggled to wrestle it open. Inside the car sat a little brown-haired boy of five or six, and his head hung limp at an odd angle. LaGrange whipped off a glove and reached for the small wrist to check for a pulse. The sounds of the pounding precipitation distracted his ears. His spirits fell again even deeper. He lifted the boy's dangling head to listen for breath. Already the child's body grew cold and inanimate.

Glancing across to the front of the car, in the passenger seat, another figure had slumped. The man flopped lifelessly like his son.

LaGrange contorted his body to climb through the broken branches engulfing the crashed sedan. Crouching low, he wrestled to rip open that remaining passenger door. As he leaned into the car to check the man's wrist for a sign of life, LaGrange snapped to attention. This one had a rhythmic pulse softly pounding below his skin. He was alive but unconscious. How long he would remain so was uncertain given the cold, brutal environment.

LaGrange checked the victim's eyes, dilated pupils in his flashlight's beam. The gravity of the situation clutched him fast. Here, at the bottom of a desolate wasteland, alone in the dark in the middle of nowhere, no witnesses, none of society's rules applied. Nothing. This opportunity was a gift. Such moments the universe did provide occasionally, if only men of science were self-aware enough to recognize their broader implications and seize their chances fully without hesitation.

"Steven Arkin," said the man's driver's license.

Why was he not driving the vehicle instead of the woman? LaGrange took mental notes, and he considered which path forward. Arkin, Steven, lay peacefully in his passenger seat without a care. But it was best if he was removed from this hostile predicament to receive proper medical assistance elsewhere. Anywhere should be better than here.

Raindrops smashed harder, knocking glass particles from the shattered windshield. LaGrange's gloved hand twisted Steven Arkin's face, and he scrutinized his new patient in the flashlight beam. Glazed-over eyes stared with blank lifelessness. This was probably the end of Steven Arkin, but he was surely worth a try, for the sake of science.

LaGrange listened again, pulling off his glove and feeling Arkin's jugular to hear the strength of the heart. Bumping regularly, like any other man, it seemed the problem was purely cognitive. Perhaps there was some hope for this Steven Arkin yet.

LaGrange flipped open his pocket knife, and he yanked out the vehicle's seat belt.

Up the slick, muddy hillside, he dragged Arkin to higher and higher elevations like a sled behind him. Slipping back down several yards and nearly tumbling over, the seasonal rainstorm flooded hard, and silt gave way underfoot like pastry.

Undeterred, the Frenchman forged up the hill

with his patient in tow. As he approached the crest, headlights flashed. LaGrange ducked down out of sight. Motionless, he checked Arkin's current condition. The white beams streaked past above him, and the engine sounds receded into the storm.

LaGrange's muddy gloves clawed into the eroding muck, challenging gravity to progress those final few steps up to the pavement. Now he was growling like a savage to haul this comatose body away with him.

At the rear of his van, he wrenched Arkin upward and into the back of the vehicle. Panting madly, like a spent animal, his hand slammed the doors shut with its precious cargo inside.

LaGrange Radio-Bio Engineering Ltd., read the back door.

Sweating bestially, LaGrange extricated himself from his hot rubber raincoat. Behind him, in the dry van, he checked that the motionless man remained. Steven Arkin, his new pet project, it was an eerie dream come to life in the world.

LaGrange poked his hand inside a brown paper bag for his flask of port. Large gulps of the liquor soothed his shaking arms. Twisting the cap back onto the bottle and swiftly turning the ignition key, LaGrange's stereo blared to life again. "Entanglement is everything," said his former self in a former time frame.

"Entanglement is the fabric of the universe. We may all be said to exist as nothing *but* a collection of entanglements..."

His white van jolted ahead into the rainstorm, while his vegetative passenger slid randomly around on the wet steel floor.

SIX

The television screen up on the yellow wall blurred so much that two screens separated in his head. D'Andre Walker's pain medication had increased. Now he felt confused, unable to choose a program worth watching. It was hard work to keep pressing the remote-controller button.

It was hard to want to stay alive. *What was the point of it all anyways?*

A blonde white lady on the TV screen said, "Good morning everybody!" She was way too happy, but really pretty.

D'Andre figured out that it must be morning. Raspberry *Jello* sat uneaten on a tray in front of him. He poked his little white spork at the red gel, and it danced around in the Styrofoam cup. He wasn't sure if he could keep it down today. The pain meds made him feel all queasy.

Up on that TV screen, some too-happy middle-aged white guy with perfect hair said, "Everyone just loves Supernatural Steven Arkin."

The pretty blonde lady smiled. "I know I do—" Then she put her hand up to her ear and whispered, "Call me, Steve."

D'Andre's interest piqued, and he focused hard to read the words crawling quickly across the bottom ticker. They showed Supernatural Steve's promotional photos and a video of him flying around with some lucky kid.

The TV man held up an envelope, and he ripped it open. "Well it's time to reveal today's lucky child, who gets a *Wish to Dream* with Supernatural Steve. We should get a drum roll—"

"We should," said the lady.

"Here it is," he said, and he held up the card. "It's D'Andre Walker of the Bronx Children's Hospital in New York City!"

D'Andre spit out his *Jello,* his face like frozen

plastic. In a haze, he gawked up at the morning show and rattled his head back and forth to wake up.

"Am I dreamin'?"

The news show placed his photograph right next to Steve Arkin's. The TV man kept talking, "D'Andre, who's ten, gets a *Wish to Dream.*"

The pretty lady cut him off, as she usually did in their morning joking around. "A *Supernatural* wish, John."

He nodded back at her. "Far out. Just, far out. Well congratulations, D'Andre, and we'll see you soon!"

Nurse Shondra rushed into the room, trailed by the other nurses. She jumped up and down. "It's you, baby! I can't believe it! Oh my God! You so lucky!"

D'Andre remained mute. In full daze, he was swept over to the rec room by the gathering of nurses. Dazzled children crowded around and tried to touch his arms.

D'Andre exited the shower steam, delirious as ever. The thick humid air hindered his breathing. He brushed his teeth, and he trudged back down the hallway to his own room. When he stepped inside, a different TV program played above.

The news anchor sounded serious.

"Shocking photographs from Bolivia this morning. These appear to show at least two Supernaturals were present at the recent clash which cost the lives of a demonstration leader as well as a four-month-old infant."

D'Andre stepped back to gaze up at the screen.

Smeared photos revealed the lower half of Barby the Barbarian flying up through a mangled tin roof. Video footage moved in toward the crushed baby, laid out on a blanket, surrounded by weeping Bolivian women.

D'Andre gasped.

Violent protesters crashed against the plastic shields of the security forces. Thousands of activists shouted and pushed signs in the air.

The TV screen said *Could Supernaturals Be Taking Sides in the Dispute?*

When the news program replayed the face of the dead baby, D'Andre turned away, grabbed his remote controller and clicked it off.

Dropping into his chair, he held his face in his hands.

Time passed.

D'Andre hadn't moved when the *Wish to Dream* spokespeople piled into his little hovel along with all the nurses, a couple of doctors, orderlies and a media circus trailing behind them so sprawled out that they filled the entire floor. Bright portable lights blinded his eyes. Cameras on tripods flashed. The clamor of competing voices swirled inside his head. D'Andre didn't figure out what to say to them.

The human tsunami whooshed him downstairs out to a waiting black limousine at the head of a procession, with vans and cops on motorcycles with their flashing red and blue strobes. Everybody tagged along after him in a line across the bridge over the river into Manhattan.

D'Andre couldn't think of anything good to say to anybody. He curled up on the leather seat, and he listened to the *Wish to Dream* lady whisper softly into a man's ear. They stared at him for the entire ride.

D'Andre closed his eyes to save his strength. He wanted to be strong enough to meet Supernatural Steve.

"How are you holding up there, kiddo?" The woman in the suit jacket smiled with a big fake grin.

D'Andre closed his eyes again, and he shrugged

back at her.

"Are you okay? Do you need anything from us? A drink? Crackers?"

He shook his head.

"You took all your pills like you're supposed to?"

He nodded. The *Wish* lady had long dark brown hair, like Mom's. He stared at her hair, and he tried to remember his Mom's face.

Their motorcade snaked into Central Park, a lush green field ringed by grey skyscrapers. Here reporters, government representatives, spectators and others gathered at a stage just above the lawn. Nurse Shondra helped D'Andre climb up the stairs, and she kept him pressed up against her thick legs.

D'Andre breathed deeply, and he watched the crowd form across the park, people streaming in from every direction to see Supernatural Steve.

Nurse Shondra jolted his shoulders. "Aww, here he comes, baby. Look, look!"

The energy of the crowd shot up toward the overcast sky, and a tiny dark speck in the distance. Above the buildings Steve was closing in on them.

D'Andre's eyes opened wide, as Steve Arkin grew larger and sailed down toward their little stage.

Arkin landed softly on the wood to the roar of the jubilant crowd. He smiled out at the people, and he pointed casually at his friends.

From the rear of the stage, D'Andre watched silently, as the full production of the show ramped-up. Everyone had their little job to do.

The *Wish to Dream* people approached him and took him by the hand. He stepped up toward Supernatural Steve at center stage, while several thousand faces bristled below, scattered across the expanse.

Steve bent low to face him. "Hey, kid. Ready to see the world?"

D'Andre stood motionless, staring. He'd never been so close to a Supernatural in his life. He had studied them in books and on the Internet, but now he was right next to Steve Arkin, and he didn't know what he was supposed to feel. Steve had a buzzing energy inside him, like he could fly away any second. It took all of D'Andre's strength to stand up straight and not shake.

The *Wish to Dream* people handed a clipboard to Steve, and he broke away to read it to the people.

D'Andre watched two Japanese businessmen in suits pose beside Steve, holding a large check.

Photographers flashed. They ignored D'Andre and they went through their script.

"All right," said Steve. "Let's do it." He clapped his hands together.

Into the microphone, Steve announced, "The gracious Michihama Corporation has developed this state of the art flight suit specifically for the *Wish to Dream* kids' flight program."

Spectators applauded as Steve showed off the stylish blue jumpsuit.

D'Andre decided to step forward, and he shuffled up and tugged on Steve's shirt sleeve.

"Hold on, kid. I'm supposed to read this. There's donations involved."

The TV cameras zoomed in on D'Andre, and they pushed in closer. Reporters leaned forward at the foot of the short stage.

D'Andre heard one of the reporters say, "What's the kid's deal?"

D'Andre watched quietly, as Steve checked the script pages.

"Michihama's high tech polymers," said Steve, "keep you warm at even 10,000 feet. It's light, aerodynamic, and includes a safety chute—actually my suggestion. They're putting bleeding edge technology to work to benefit—"

D'Andre shouted over the loudspeakers, "I don't want to fly!"

The entire park fell silent.

"Wha-?" Supernatural Steve turned to look down on him.

D'Andre huffed in a bout of confusion. "That's not my dream. That's not my wish." His body trembled slightly at the center of the world, but his face remained determined.

The cameras clicked in rapid fire. Everyone focused their attention on little D'Andre Walker.

Supernatural Steve knelt down at D'Andre's level. "It's not?"

Reporters jotted notes. Camera phones recorded the exchange. The crowd simmered, as the video went out live internationally.

Steve re-positioned himself. "What is your wish, young man?"

D'Andre shouted out at the crowd, "There was Supernaturals. They killed the baby. It's on da news. They wasn't heroes. They wasn't heroes."

Steven Arkin flinched. "I see."

Television crews leaned in closer.

D'Andre spun back and forth, almost out of breath. "Use your powers and make it right. That the Supernaturals are heroes. Not bad guys."

Steve froze.

Cameras continued to roll.

He didn't respond.

A reporter said, "Did you catch that?"

"What's he saying?"

"Just heroes," said D'Andre Walker. "Only."

SEVEN

Steven Arkin accompanied D'Andre Walker in the limousine, as they drove back across the bridge to the Bronx. The boy didn't speak further. He seemed fatigued.

Steve worried, believing something larger than all of them had just happened. He was unsure how to respond, now that the incident had gone out globally on television signals. Not just humanity, but the Supernatural realm would also have instantly noticed.

He and the boy slowly walked into the children's hospital, surrounded by the medical staff and the media entourage, and even the patients who crowded to catch a glimpse of the big show. It was a massive, confused frenzy. Steve followed after the boy to the elevator, waving at everyone and smiling for photos.

D'Andre carried his little travel tote bag. When they reached his personal room he unpacked his meager belongings, an extra shirt, underwear, jacket, hat, gloves.

Steve sat down silently on the room's chair, as the boy climbed back up into his freshly made bed.

A nurse placed an oxygen mask on the boy and then exited.

Steve closed the door behind her. "What you're asking is... I don't know. I don't actually have any power in the *Council*. Do you understand what that means?"

"No," said the boy.

"I can't make any decisions for other Supernaturals."

D'Andre glanced over.

"I've only been powered up for three years, kid. Those are ancient, I don't know, beings. I don't even know if they're originally from this planet. Do you understand? I've seen things—"

"Like what?"

"Things that give me pause. Listen. No sane person would oppose—."

"So get a little crazy." D'Andre chortled and turned away. He grabbed for his remote controller and powered on his TV.

Steve sighed. "It's just not done. I don't know how to put this."

On the TV screen above them, their park press conference replayed. A news anchorman spoke over all of their words and attempted to spin the meaning into something else. He said, "What to make of this little D'Andre Walker's odd statements this afternoon?"

Steve shook his head. "Kid? Kid? Turn that down, will ya? I'm trying to think."

D'Andre lowered the volume, but he kept watching. He whispered, "That's my wish. You don't gotta do it. Whateva."

Steve gritted his teeth. "Hey? What's your name?"

"You don't remember?"

He shrugged. "I see a lot of people in a day, kid—"

"D'ANDRE WALKER!!!"

Steve froze. "I'm sorry. Where are your parents? They couldn't make it off work or something?"

D'Andre huffed out. "Or suttom."

Steve rose and strolled uncomfortably to the

sixth floor window. Down below, the media scurried in full buzz, news vans and camera people. He peeked out of the narrow glass of the room's door. Numerous others chatted and waited for the two to emerge.

D'Andre stewed, his face turned to the side. He clicked off his lamp. Dismal cloudy daylight flickered across the blanket.

Steve spun back with conviction. "Look, D'Andre. I don't believe a Supernatural killed a baby. I mean why would they? It doesn't make any sense. The news could be wrong you know?"

D'Andre turned to him. "They overthrew the president East Africa right? Started a civil war?"

"Now I don't know anything about that."

"I saw the news. Shouldn't you know about that?"

Steve pulled open the window, just enough to escape through. He floated up gently from the floor. "I'll look into it. Okay? I'll tell you what I find out."

D'Andre jolted up in bed. "Okay."

Steve sailed gingerly up and out the portal, but he whipped back as he hovered outside. "And you listen to your doctors. Take it easy, D'Andre."

D'Andre flicked to another channel.

Steve shot off over the Bronx, as reporters below filmed him. He soared high away from everyone, above the grimy cityscape and its myriad problems. His partial memory remained full of holes of what his life used to be prior to his transmogrification. He remembered his skin smoldering, steam escaping every pore. Heat ripped from his molecules. From the deep blackness his body jolted again to consciousness, but it was a new state of being. He had found a multidimensional reality, a dark, invisible universe coursing straight through our own and overlapping it.

The first thing Steve had realized, once reawakened, was that he was strapped down to a bed and immobile. The room around him was stuffed with medical monitoring devices, most of them smashed, fallen about from some earthquake event. Machines beeped, displaying numbers and squiggly lines.

All his pain receded into the ether as if flushed away into another dimension. Perhaps it was his mind that receded from this world into the next. His eyes wiggled, and he spotted a man in a lab coat stumbling toward him with a syringe in one hand. Like a shuffling corpse the lab coat man was blackened from fire and smoke. His skin was painted in burns and boils, as if from an overdose of radiation.

The lab man inspected the working machines, and he limped closer to Steve, who was still strapped down. His latex-gloved fingers prodded Steve's eyelids apart and blinded him with a penlight.

Steve wrenched against the straps. "What have you done to me?"

The seared face struggled to form a smile, but his skin had solidified in its carbonized deformations. Above Steve's cot, the scientist teetered, barely able to remain standing.

His hair dropped out as he spoke, "What have I done? Monsieur Guinea Pig?"

Steve tried to slide away from the decaying, ghoulish face, but he was held fast by thick, leather restraints.

The deformed man snickered knowingly.

"I've transmuted you from a scrap of dead meat, into the most glorious specimen homo sapiens in all human history." He attempted to laugh, but he coughed up dark blood instead.

That was all Steve could remember of his interaction with his creator.

A 767 passenger jet pitched radically to avoid

smashing into him. The massive jet engine whooshed past and spun him like a top. Terrified passengers at their windows. Steve awoke, embarrassed at his carelessness, somehow drifted into the plane landing corridor. He soared off west, bolting high and away from the air traffic lanes.

Steve's suburban house remained unknown to the general public. Just another box squeezed in among the thousands. He avoided notice by driving that final half-mile and pulling quickly into his garage. Several neighbors kept his identity confidential. They preferred to have him nearby, in case they ever needed his assistance.

Steve fired up his computer and television set, tossed in a microwave dinner, popped open a beer, and he went to work researching the many issues bouncing around in his skull.

What immediately seized his attention was the otherworldly, feminine voice of Miss Melt, Pandora, swirling up and out from his television speakers. She beamed from the *Late News* show. Cameras couldn't process her incredible energy fields, which she constantly emitted. She gleamed in a strange rainbow of light.

"Thanks Brett, for giving me this opportunity to clarify just what happened."

Steve jumped close to watch her on the TV.

Pandora hypnotized like a mystical angel goddess speaking straight from her heart. There was something captivating in everything she did. She melted away his capacity for logic.

The news anchor, Brett, gawked from across his desk. "We just love having you here, Miss Melt. So what is the real story that everyone should know?"

A photo appeared. A pair of massive, unmistakable legs, Barby the Barbarian flew up through a hole in a tin roof.

Pandora's fine hair glowed, her energy fibers searing the camera's sensor.

"While it's true," she said, "that Supernaturals were present at the meeting in question, they were in no way responsible for any of the violence."

Brett Holt, the news show's host, said, "Do you have any further evidence to convince our viewers?"

Pandora faced down the camera in close-up. Her glowing violet eyes peered. Luminous hair swayed back and forth like the tide. "The *Council of Power* is currently investigating this matter, but it seems very clear to us that the culprits behind this atrocity were quite human."

"You've discovered their identities?"

She half-nodded in the affirmative. "Our heroes raced down to protect the people from those radical insurgent elements in their little protest movement."

"I take it that they were unsuccessful?"

She nodded. "It was very messy, and the Supernaturals apparently arrived too late to have saved the two victims. We can't be everywhere."

The host assumed a somber tone. His camera pushed in tightly. "It's tragic, truly, that they weren't in time. Thank you for appearing here Miss Melt. It is always a pleasure. And you are always welcome back."

"Thank you, Brett, for doing great journalism and getting the story straight."

The host sprang taller in his chair. "Next up: pre-school fat farms?"

Steve clicked to a different channel and hunted through the news stations for further coverage.

Mark Traynor plastered Steve's face up on his screen. "This shocking footage from SkyAir 7669 this afternoon. Could that be? Of course! We zoom in and see the unknowable Steven Arkin obstructing the landing path on the approach into LaGuardia Airport! What in the hell is going on, Steve? Terrorized passengers, as the jet needed to make an abrupt emergency evasive maneuver. There he is. How about an explanation, Mr. Arkin, endangering human lives so glibly?"

Steve sighed, and he reached for his phone.

"Yes. Please put me through to the network's switchboard. Thank you."

When his voice finally routed into the studio, Mark Traynor was still in mid-rant. "Do we need our military to more actively police our skies? Is that what it's... wait a minute. We have Steven Arkin on the line?"

"Hello Mark."

"Is this you, Steve?"

"Yes it is, and I'm very sorry to all those passengers for my moment of, uh, carelessness."

"Well, buddy," said the pundit, with sarcasm, "you should be in a lot of doggie doo doo, if you know what I'm saying. How do you explain nearly taking out an airliner like that? Right over New York City!"

"It's inexcusable."

"Yeah. That's right. Steve, I mean, you need to do something, make some changes to make this right."

Steve stared at the image of Traynor's arrogant,

admonishing face.

"You need to come down here to this studio and let's sort out some priorities, right here on the air."

"Hhhhhh." Steve demurred.

"We can definitely have you in," continued Traynor. "Tomorrow night. What do you say? Let's set the record straight and really get into it."

Steve shook his head. "Well I'm not going to do that."

Traynor scoffed. "Well you owe—"

"I'm not going to legitimize your network, Mark, or the ideology you pump out twenty-four hours a day. So, no. I'm not going to go in there in person."

Traynor threw up his hands. "So screw the people, now that you're above all of us?"

"You're not *the people*, Mr. Traynor. I can apologize to those passengers right now."

"Whom you terrorized."

"That's a completely wrong word. No. A loaded word and you know it." Steve huffed. "I can tell all those passengers on that flight, and the crew, that I am truly sorry that I was careless today. I had a lot on my mind, and I know that's no excuse. I vow to be more vigilant in the future, and to stay one step ahead of circumstances, as best I can."

"Is that it?"

"Yeah Mark. If anyone affected would like to speak to me further they can contact me themselves. They don't need you as a middleman."

Steve clicked off his TV, and he flicked through the Internet's crude photographs of the Bolivian incident. He found nothing conclusive.

He slurped down the rest of his beer. Several empty bottles sat on his desk. Late night, he turned off his computer, and he trudged off to his bed. Atop his dresser sat photographs of his son Michael at the park and at the beach. A single image of Cathy, their wedding photograph, remained hanging on the wall.

Steve brushed his teeth, and he dove into his oversized bed to sleep another night alone.

EIGHT

A massive salvage ship sat in the sun in the endless North Atlantic.

Steve Arkin floated down and landed on a narrow deck, which wrapped around the bridge. Feet on steel beside the railing, he peeked about the enormous vessel and then proceeded to stroll in through a hatch.

Sinewy sailors, scientists, and officers held motionless as Steve entered their control room. The wrinkled captain extended his hand. "Mr. Arkin, a good mornin' to ya."

"Thanks, cap."

"You'd like any coffee? Donuts?" The captain pointed toward the breakfast table, where the muscular guys covertly stuffed themselves.

"Yeah. Don't mind if I do. Gentlemen."

The men stepped aside. All studied Steve's breakfast choices.

A coffee cup and a half donut left on the sea chart, Steve lifted the stack of contract papers. It was time to try and understand the long-winded legalese.

"It's the Lloyd's standard," said the captain. "If that's okay with you, Mr. Arkin? We weren't all that certain what your requirements would be."

Annoyed and confused at the wordiness of the agreement, Steve gave up trying. "So how deep is it?"

"She's four-thousand four-hundred, and twenty-two."

"Feet?"

"Meters."

Steve rolled his eyes. About to sign on the dotted line, his hand paused. "Should I be worried? Is this thing leaking radiation?"

The scientists snapped behind him in the shadows but they kept their silence. Steve sensed their minutest fluctuations in body chemistry. Their signals didn't portend good news.

The captain quickly shrugged. "We don't really

know."

Steve assessed the workmen around the room for signs of deceit. He huffed out, waving his pen. "So why hasn't the Navy done it?"

"Doubt they care, Mr. Arkin. Cold War's over."

Steve snatched up the papers for a final glance. He'd never attempted to dive to such a depth before, and he wasn't sure it was even possible. He had no inkling of what would occur if he failed to fulfill the written agreement. Unwilling to show those characters any timidity, he just signed the documents and initialed pages.

Outside, on the sprawling specialized deck, the air felt warm and easy. Sky blue, scattered puffs, and the sea's glassy surface softly swayed.

Steve grabbed the collared end of a thick steel cable in one hand and a heavy sealed light in the other. The leash fed back endlessly onto a massive roller mounted to a superstructure high above.

A bearded sea dog nodded in Steve's direction. "All in a day's work, huh, Arkin?"

He positioned himself. "Give me about an hour."

Deck hands watched in curious amusement.

Steve dove over the side of the ship and down

into the blue depths, yanking the steel cable behind him as fast as it would unspool. Temperature no longer bothered him, and he wasn't certain why. He quickly passed from light to darkness. His own light ignited, but it was of little use poking into the black void below. He soared downward toward the earth's center in a tunnel of black water.

Squeaks from a passing whale echoed in his head. Surface turbulence receded to silence. His journey progressed without incident until the white sandy ocean floor suddenly appeared in his light beam.

A luminescent fish circled lazily, drawn toward the light.

Steve twisted about on the ocean bottom, searching in the limited range of the beam. Nothing.

Kicking off again, he spiraled out away until suddenly there it was jutting up from the bottom, bent structural damage, and a crack in the hull. Its nose buried in the sea floor, its grey metal skin held faded Cyrillic writing. The submarine seemed to vibrate the surrounding water with subtle energy waves.

Steve suspected plutonium or uranium had breached their containments. Alone on the endless ocean floor with the Soviet wreck, Steve maneuvered the steel cable to wrap it around the hull several times. When that satisfied him, he locked the collar at the sub's midsection, just below the conning tower.

Swimming back up from the pulsing radiation, he was ready to call it a day's work, but he had to be sure. Back down to the sea floor, he pushed and yanked at the embedded submarine to loosen it up. The boat crashed with a massive ejection of sand squirting out in all directions. Then it lay flat and lifeless on the bottom.

Steve dropped the light and flew back up to the world at top speed.

Landing on the salvage ship's deck, he paused in a moment of confusion. All those scientists now wore haz-mat suits from head to toe and measured him with a Geiger counter, which clicked rapidly. They guided him into a shower stall, which had been readied on the deck.

The haz-mat guys hosed him down and instructed him to scrub. After a couple extra scrubbings, with brushes on long sticks, Steve passed their Geiger tests. He wrapped himself in a towel and emerged from the temporary stall. Locating the winch operator, he called out, "I loosened it up for ya."

Creaks snapped from that immense cable. The

tension flexed and sent out ghostly rumbles across the sea. Sailors hid themselves behind steel barriers just in case. Slowly, their machine reeled in the catch, rotations and rotations.

Steve dressed himself in a spare outfit. With a half-hearted wave he returned to the sky, leaving the clean-up job for the company to handle. His job was complete.

Steve decided to drop back to earth in an alley between looming skyscrapers. He felt satisfied that no one saw him arrive. Spectators could be so problematic.

Stepping out into the city's bright glare, he nearly stumbled through a plate glass wall panel being carried by four workmen. "Whoa! Hey fellas."

He smiled and located the immediate building entrance. From his hand-scribbled note he verified the address.

Behind him, the plate glass shattered into a million pieces. A sonic boom rocked the sky above and shook the entire avenue. Steve peered up to catch a streak of blur shoot from the penthouse above him. The sound bubble blasted and set off car alarms across the already noisy midtown district. Pedestrians covered their heads, rattled by the shock waves.

Within the polished silver elevator Steve comported himself stoically. The box rocketed up toward that same penthouse suite. He strode out into the hallway to find a set of double doors.

Instantly, the two doors parted on their own.

Miss Melt strolled out in a long gown to greet him, bathed in an effervescent green glow.

Her energy dazzled his eyes, and he blinked uncontrollably. "Hello."

"Steven," she said, her bright resonance rolling off the walls. "It didn't take you long."

"Pardon me?"

"To drop by."

"Oh. No. Nice to see you, Pandora."

"You don't sound so enthralled."

"I am. It's just hard to focus my eyes."

"Am I bubbling?" She giggled at the ceiling and toned down her emission. "Entrée."

Steve stepped cautiously inside her suite, as she led him through a maze. The loft overflowed with jungle plants stacked on multiple levels. Cautious to avoid glancing at her ass, Steve studied the gargantuan red flowers instead. Such strange shapes jutted in layers toward the ceiling high above. Her penthouse space was enormous and covered the entire building's footprint. Two stories high, with a row of windows above them, the late-day sunshine poured onto her miniature indoor rain forest.

"Would you like a drink?" she asked. "Hors d'oeuvres?"

"No thank you. I ate already. You don't have to."

Pandora fumbled behind her bar. Martini glasses clanked as she retrieved them from an overhead rack.

"Well, something, Steve. I like to play hostess when I get the chance." Pandora's skin had turned pale orange, like some movie character.

"Of course," said Steve. "Whatever you're having is fine with me."

"That's better." Her iridescent hair lightened in hue to a soft angelic gold as she turned away from him.

Steve spied around the couches and structures buried throughout the creeping jungle plants. His eyes widened pleasantly.

"Pandora?"

"Mmm?" She tossed a green olive into his martini. When her eyes again appeared, she slid silently around the bar with a glass in each hand.

Steve stood firm. "Before I came up, there was an

incident, somebody moving at high speed. Did you see them?"

"Oh." She shrugged dismissively. "That's just Stellar delivering correspondence. You know. He's a glorified mailman."

"Ah."

She held up her martini. Steve carefully clanked his. They sipped.

"What's on your mind, Steven?" Her body climbed gracefully onto her plush couch, while gulping from her glass. Her hair adjusted toward the magenta color of the fabric, like a chameleon who couldn't help but constantly evolve to circumstances.

Yellow cat eyes glared out from the dark shadows beneath the wide green leaves.

Steve peeked curiously around the lush garden. "Do you have some sort of a box that I should be aware of?"

Pandora deflated, her face disgusted. "I am the vessel, Steven."

He twitched. "Oh! I'm sorry. Did I offend you?"

Pandora huffed and downed her remaining cocktail. "No. It's just. It's always the same. I so despise clichés."

He leaned in toward her. "I so apologize. Can I make it up to you somehow?"

She whipped her fiery head back. "What did you have in mind?"

"Um. We could go. Go to the movies or something?"

"The movies? Huh!" Giddy with amusement, she laughed and squirmed with delight, colors of the rainbow spilling in random patterns across her hair and face.

Steve shrugged. "Dinner?"

NINE

Garbage cans and stray cats littered about the dark city alley, Steve Arkin dropped down silently. Marching around the corner, he claimed a spot in front of the entrance to the *Majestic Cinema*. Gazing at the gathered patrons and as nervous as a schoolboy, but she was nowhere in sight. He felt powerless, momentarily, because he wanted so much more of her, like the rest of them, like any other man. She was indescribable with some kind of internal magic force that worked on his brain like an addiction.

"Boo." Above his hair, Pandora's bare foot flicked at the top of his head. She floated like a ballerina, descending swiftly to face him in the parting sea of bedazzled moviegoers. Onlookers reached for their cell phones to video the two Supernaturals together.

"Subtle," said Steve, unable to rein in his smile. Her ambient glow lit up the sidewalk.

"Oh?" she said, "Was that a prerequisite?" Pandora's skin lightened from pale blue to almost white. She floated several inches off the concrete to remain at eye level with him.

"No. Of course not. As you wish."

Flashes popped. The pair stood surrounded by the stunned crowd.

Pandora smiled casually. Her hair flickered and adjusted. "Well I'm ready for the big movie show. What is this film, anyway?"

The two Supernaturals strolled through the cinema entrance, mobbed by random Tweeters taking selfies and sending them off somewhere.

The theater's manager approached them and beckoned them in. "Come. Come right this way."

Steve smiled and nodded to the spectators. "Uh. Popcorn? I'm not even sure. Do you eat?"

Pandora spun aimlessly. "Sure. What the hell? Gimme the whole Hollywood experience, Stevo."

By midpoint of the film, the audience had

saddened at the death of a beloved mother. Tears fell. Violins surged. The crowd mostly forgot about the two Supernaturals sitting together in the center of the room.

Pandora gaily stuffed her mouth with popcorn. Amused at all the emotion, she giggled loudly.

Beside her, Steve gawked at the screen in silence.

Pandora crunched popcorn. "Mmm, mmm." She reached across Steve's lap, grabbed the cup of soda from his armrest and loudly slurped down the remainder. A few loud extra slurps for effect, and she laughed to the ceiling. The audience sat stoically on the verge of tears, as the funeral proceeded on the screen. Pandora turned to Steve, but he whipped away to hide a tear on his cheek.

"Hey?" She playfully poked at his elbow. "Hey? Steeeeeeve? Are you crying?" She cackled.

A distant "Shhhh!"

"Shush yourself!" Pandora unwrapped the tinfoil from a chocolate bar, as the audience sat transfixed at the screen. Swallowing the bar whole, she wiped her lips on the sleeve of her dress. "You people didn't see that coming a mile away?"

"Shhhhhhhh!"

Steve slid lower in his seat to avoid breaking out

in his own nervous laughter. Pandora fidgeted beside him.

After the film ended on a positive note, the crowd poured out into the lobby. People resumed their rubbernecking and photography.

Pandora raised her voice above their cacophony. "You're a real sucker for that stuff, huh?"

Steve nodded. "I guess I am."

Arm in arm, through the theater's doors, they exited. News reporters arrived outside. Glaring lights blinded. Foreign tourists along the sidewalk jumped back and reached for their phones.

Steve held his palms up. "We should probably—"

He turned back to find Pandora, but she had already shot up into the hazy city sky.

Steve bolted after her. She led him around the avenues to her own tower. A large mechanical window tilted open, and the two Supers flew straight inside to land together in her loft garden.

Pandora's head angled. "Time for a drink?"

"I, uh. Guess I don't mind."

She grabbed ice and glasses. Her aquamarine tint warmed up toward pink. She tended to glow in winter colors unless she made some effort to blend in.

Pandora poured out a concoction and shook it briskly with ice. "Thanks for taking me to the arty movie."

"Pandora?"

"Yes?"

Steve stood motionless. "Can I ask you what they found out about that incident that happened in Bolivia?"

"Oh." She stopped cold. "Uh. Not much." Her hair glowed brighter with surreal shimmers that trailed off behind her like a tail.

Steve's eyes widened, mesmerized by her energy show.

Pandora came forward, and she handed him another glass.

"Um. The investigation is closed?"

She gulped down half of her tall glass, dribbling a bit across her jaw. "Well I really don't know. Dragomir probably knows more about it than I do."

Steve guzzled his entire cocktail in one gulp. "Okay. Well thanks for the drink. I'll ask him then."

Her arms folded, and she huffed out. "Arkin, why are you such a downer?"

"Am I?"

"Of course you are."

"Well, thanks."

She flopped down onto her couch. "Probably hung up on your mortal tribulations. Old news."

"Perhaps. So, uhh. What was that secret you were so hot to tell me?"

"Hot?" Her eyes darted over him. She paused for a moment. "My secret? Oh! He does listen."

Steve folded his arms. "Well, go on."

"What's in it for me?"

"You brought it up."

"Not this time, darling. But fine. You really want to know?" She perked up tall, sitting across on the opposite couch. "What if I were to tell you that I was bored and I tinkered with your DNA."

Steve jolted. "My DNA? How?" He patted himself down and examined his torso.

Her laughter ricocheted off the walls and swirled like a cyclone around the massive space. Steve felt his nervous system plummet from her pummeling vibrations.

"No." She scoffed. "Not you. Stupid. The whole planet. You see, I brought a few alien samples back with me, to mix it up a bit. This was millions of years ago."

"Millions?"

"A billion?" She flailed her head about playfully. "I don't know. Who cares really? But it was me. You're welcome."

"You visited other planets?"

Her eyes glowed in pearly white. "Well, duh."

"And they had life?"

"Crummy, slimy things, yeah, plenty."

"Okay."

Yellow light oozed from her pores. "So what are you hiding, Steven? You know you'll tell me eventually."

"Nothing." He shook his head. "Certainly nothing on that scale."

"Then scale it down. Come on, Arkin. Spill."

He bowed slightly as he stepped back. "I really need to go."

"Oh?" she murmured, with surprise. "Drop by anytime, Steve." Her grin danced in an increasingly hazy glow. She seemed determined about something.

Steve flew up and out through the overhead window egress. Arcing over the twinkling city, he found his bearings on a trajectory toward the stratosphere.

The Himalaya range was raked by the sunrise skipping delicately across white peaks to the horizon. Infrared lights flickered in the windows of the massive stone palace fortress below. Steve descended to the front entrance chamber, where he found himself quite alone and facing the massive sealed door. He pressed the electronic doorbell.

Dragomir himself appeared at once on the security screen. "Yes? Mr. Arkin, what can I do for you?"

Steve stepped inside the *Council* fortress and through several long hallways toward the Presidential suite.

Dragomir welcomed him in the doorway. The interim President wore Gungnir, that silver spear, strapped awkwardly across his back, his wings twitching to situate themselves comfortably. Blue sparks and sheen leaked constantly from the long weapon.

The Presidential chamber was originally carved into an enormous stone cavern. Grecco-Roman columns featured alongside more recent technological upgrades.

"Steven Arkin. How are you, my friend?"

"I'm okay."

"Sit. Sit will you?" Dragomir placed the long spear into a holder beside his chair.

"Sure."

Dragomir took his own chair with symmetrical

intent, beside a massive communication workstation which took up a wall.

"So. That sick boy put you into a bit of an awkward spot, and you seek guidance."

Steve nodded. "Something like that."

Dragomir rattled on fluently, as if rehearsed, "Well here's what you could say: we–the Supers–are working with *Water Corp.* to bring clean, fresh water to those ungrateful people. When work is completed, they'll have nothing further to protest against. Problem solved."

"All right." Steve reclined in his chair to process. "But I'd like to talk to Barby and Mr. Nukeman, if I could."

"Why?" Dragomir's leathery nose curled subtly.

"Or, I could perhaps see your investigation, so I can tell D'Andre Walker and the humans of course, the news people, what you've found out."

Dragomir peered without emotion. "Ah. Well, I asked the two what happened. They told me. That's our investigation."

Steve scurried back down the long hallway into the shadows of the fortress to the exit. The tall Presidential office door latched shut behind him with an echoing thud.

TEN

Miles of stopped automobiles stretched south into Tijuana, Mexico, all of them halted by the border crossing station. A long-haired American, on foot, Rick Jenkins, stepped along the narrow walkway toward the border checkpoint. He carried only a faded olive-colored rucksack. His clothes were wrinkled and dirty, as was he.

Jenkins paused before the dark, reflective glass. He pushed his hair to one side, and he yanked open the door. The air-conditioned building felt nearly deserted despite the influx of automobiles waiting outside.

He charged in toward the metal detectors. He

knew that the TSA and ICE agents always distrusted him and his appearance. They invariably assumed he was a smuggler, and they gave him the business when he tried to return home from abroad.

Jenkins retrieved a small flash card from his green sack. He watched the border cops scrutinize his every motion.

"Good morning," said the jarhead. "Everything in the tray, please."

"Look," said Jenkins, "I don't want this damaged by the x-rays. You can check it by hand." He held the card softly out in front of him.

The officer postured aggressively, tapped his shoulder radio. "Assistance please."

A squad of border cops, male and female, led Rick Jenkins around a tall blind.

The oldest cop said, "Strip."

Rick watched them chemical swab the now highly-suspect data card. A supervisor carried a laptop computer to a workstation and inserted the card.

"Hey! That's private, man."

The TSA officer ignored him, but stiffened quickly. "There's a password."

"That's right, there's a password. It's personal.

Like I just said."

"Put your password in."

"No."

All the agents stood solemnly around him in a circle.

The young border officer grimaced. "If you don't put in your password, you're not advancing past this point."

Rick studied the young martinet. "Well I guess I'll just call my NETWORK, and have them find out who your boss is. Seems like the only thing to do."

Their demeanor changed instantly. The junior cop sailed off out of sight.

Just north of the border checkpoint, Rick hailed a taxi, jumped in, and sped off onto the freeway.

A bustling editorial news center crackled with communications. In the heart of Los Angeles, every cubicle was full, and the screens around the walls flickered with realtime updates.

Rick Jenkins shook hands with Bob Sturgett, a familiar producer. Bob was balding and chubby with a cinnamon bun in one hand and an extra-large coffee in the other.

"Morning, Rick," said Sturgett appreciatively.

"What have you got for us?"

Rick nodded, and the two men set off through the studio. Past dozens of reporters and yammering phone calls, they snaked around the perimeter of the news floor. Into a quiet video editing booth, Jenkins said nothing as he loaded up the footage.

Sturgett watched the scene unfold on the screen, and Rick studied his face. Soon Bob paused the video to place a rushed telephone call.

Rick fidgeted in the dimly lit editing bay, as Bob held up a be-patient finger. The decision came swiftly enough. Sturgett ejected the memory card and handed it back to Jenkins.

"I'm sorry, Rick. We can't touch it."

"You're sorry? That's it?"Rick stared back with disbelief.

"That's it today, man. Like I said, we're sorry."

Rick shook his head, and he pocketed the memory card. "Yeah. The network feels sorrow."

Jenkins stepped out of the lobby and into the cacophony of the avenue, alone in the shadows of the soulless skyscrapers. Across the stopped traffic lay another towering network headquarters. He timed his move and jogged through the cars over to *SharpNews 5.*

Sun falling, Rick stopped at a Gyro stand on the sidewalk, and he bought himself dinner. An electronics store featured a full window of television screens, which suited him. He approached to watch the *Channel 5* broadcast.

A pretty brunette teleprompter reader appeared. "*SharpNews Five* has acquired new video evidence pertaining to that Bolivia/Supernaturals story."

Rick chewed at the fringes of his Gyro, staring intently.

The screen lit up. Barby the Barbarian and Mr. Nukeman stood at the front of the Bolivian water protest meeting. It quickly cut away.

"Which confirms," she continued, "what we already knew. That Supernaturals arrived too late to stop the violence."

"What!!!" Sour cream dressing slopped down the front of his shirt. "Dammit." Rick Jenkins patted himself with napkins.

"And now *SportsFocus*, the hardest-hitting baseball coverage in town!"

Rick twisted nervously, and he stepped fast along the city sidewalk. At the first Internet café he found, he darted inside to claim a workstation. His flash drive at the ready, he called up the "Webleaks" information website.

ELEVEN

A bright new day and Steve soared over toward D'Andre Walker's hospital window on the sixth floor of the Bronx Children's Medical Center. Arriving at the smudged window, he tapped on the glass and startled the young patient.

He held up a white paper bag, and he hovered patiently for D'Andre to struggle out of bed and come unlock the window.

Steve floated in, and he presented the paper bag. "My favorite, when I was a kid."

D'Andre jolted. "What is it?"

"Banana split, vanilla, chocolate, strawberry, hot

fudge."

"Oooh." D'Andre ripped into the dessert like a hungry animal.

Steve strolled over to sit and relax in the room's chair. "Guess what?"

"Mmm?" D'Andre had already smeared ice cream and fudge across his jaw.

Steve grinned. "I talked directly to the President of the *Council of Power*, Dragomir. And he told me the two Supers arrived late after the violence happened. They are extremely sorry that they couldn't save the baby in time."

D'Andre dropped his spoon to the floor. A tear rolled down his cheek.

"What?" said Steve.

The boy set the banana split onto his rolling tray table. "Come here." D'Andre called with his hand as he passed through the door and out into the adjoining hallway. He led Steve through the hospital ward toward the recreation room. There, he stepped up behind another boy who was seated at a computer station playing a shooting game.

D'Andre tapped him on the shoulder. He pointed back at Steve, and the kid on the computer jumped in his seat.

"We need this," said D'Andre, and he guided Steve around to the small chair to sit. With the mouse he called up the Webleaks site, and he clicked on a new video, the "UNEDITED FOOTAGE: SUPERNATURALS STORM WATER MEETING."

Steve watched apprehensively.

D'Andre pushed over a well-worn pair of headphones.

Steve watched the footage play. It was from the day.

In the video, the reporter Rick Jenkins filmed inside a large corrugated tin structure. Steve wasn't familiar with him or who he worked for. The simple building filled quickly with rural Bolivian peasants. Jenkins interviewed people in Spanish and filmed their reactions. The lens focused and panned around the room. Villagers took their seats. Mothers carried babies in wicker baskets, which they lined up along the side wall, and left them to sleep.

This meeting hall crowded to capacity. Food was provided on tables at the rear. Jenkins grabbed his own plate and filmed it. A demonstration leader took the microphone in hand and began speaking. His hair was greying and his voice soft-spoken.

The leader pointed into Jenkin's camera lens. "I like to say some English, so Americanos know we no want *Water Corp.*"

A banner of solidarity hung on the wall behind him. He stepped up to the camera. "They take all Bolivia's water. Sell thirty dollars a month."

Rick Jenkins filmed.

"Bolivia people only make sixty dollars in a month. Is too much. They make illegal to take rain off the roof and collect in a tank. Illegal have water from the sky! This government no represent the people."

An earthquake crashed.

Ceiling timbers caved in dropping all around in a a mad panic. Dust puffed out over the heads of everyone. People scrambled and shouted to retreat from the point of impact.

Rick Jenkins yanked his camera from his tripod and retreated back out of the way, continuing to record the disruption.

Barby the Barbarian and Mr. Nukeman stomped to land at the front of the meeting room. Instant panic overcame the villagers, fear across their faces as they cowered.

The demonstration leader stood tall at the front between the Supers and the group. He held motionless to face down the two intruders. Jenkins filmed the scene covertly from the back of the crowd, ducking down low.

Mr. Nukenan stepped forward pointing his finger. "You are on the list!"

The man shrugged, not comprehending. "Que list?"

Barby jerked forward, his hulking form overshadowing everything. "THE LIST YOU DON'T WANT TO BE ON!"

Barby pounced over and grabbed the professor, lifted him angrily with one hand by the throat.

Nukeman's hot yellow eyes glowed demon-like. He berated the gathered crowd of Bolivians. "Don't follow criminals! *Banditos!*"

A lone woman stood up in the back row. Her voice crackled, "Mi husband es no criminal! He's a good man!"

This challenge enraged the Barbarian. "No he ain't!"

Barby hurled the demonstration leader across

the entire hall, over the tables, and his body crashed into the far wall, landing hard.

The stunned crowd gasped in shock. Babies cried.

Women dashed over to roll over the demonstration leader.

People waited for word.

"Aaaaaaaaa!"

The man lay motionless, his neck bent sideward.

A second woman pulled a mangled wicker basket from beneath his body. She shouted and pointed, "Bebé!"

"Es el bebé muerto?"

Barby laughed at his handiwork.

"Baby?" Nukenan listened in on the disturbance.

Jenkins whipped the camera back and forth to get a view.

The Barbarian whispered to Nukeman, "Hell are they talking about?"

Jenkins froze in place, and he turned his body to the rear of the room away from the Supers. Silently, he ejected his memory card and he slid it down his back. Inserting a fresh card, he turned back to continue filming.

A peasant woman held up the dead baby for everyone to see. Women panicked to retrieve their babies. The men rushed in to give aid.

Mr. Nukeman spotted Jenkins and his camera in the pandemonium. He tugged at Barby's arm, and the two stomped over, shoving stragglers out of their path.

Nukeman snatched the video camera from Rick's hands. He threw it down onto the dirt floor. From his eyes yellow energy beamed out and melted the machine until it became liquid and flame.

Nukeman and Barby stared angrily down on Jenkins.

Nukeman floated up toward the ceiling hole and shouted over the heads of the crowd, "From now on you drink *Water Corp's* water!"

Barby pointed an admonishing finger at the devastated villagers. "Don't make us come back here to this dump."

Barby and Mr. Nukeman rocketed up through the roof hole. As they did, a teenaged boy snapped a couple of photos with his cell phone.

Jenkins hyperventilated and his hands shook.

Supernatural Steve gazed at the Webleaks video as it ended, in the Children's Hospital recreation room.

His hands removed the headphones, and he looked back for D'Andre.

The kid sat silently in the corner scraping up the last remains of his ice cream sundae. The other children of the ward squeezed in around to spectate.

Steve nodded back toward the hallway. "Let's talk about this." He stepped carefully past the kids, nodding at them like Gulliver among the Lilliputians. "Hi there."

The two reentered D'Andre's personal room.

Steve shut the door. "I'll tell President Dragomir."

D'Andre shook his head exasperated. "You don't think he knows?"

"I really don't know." Steve found his palms up, outstretched and pathetic.

"Well I do!" D'Andre seemed pissed off. "Don't trust Dragomir, Steve. He a creepy ass gangsta. Anybody could see dat." D'Andre climbed back up into his bed.

Steve inhaled at length. "Look. Appearances aren't everything, D'Andre. Especially when it comes to Supernaturals."

The boy shrugged back. "What about Woden? Where he go?"

"Valhalla. I assume."

D'Andre shook his head. "Everything changed after Woden's gone! So who's in charge now?"

"Look, I can't assume things about President Dragomir. I need to be cautious."

D'Andre rolled his eyes. "Well you can't assume he innocent neither! My momma said don't trust nobody with power. What they do to get it? How far they go to keep it? That's what she said."

"You know," said Steve, "I would like to have a chat with your mother, actually."

"Don't you know nuthin?" D'Andre covered his eyes with his hand. "She dead! They both dead!"

Steve stood up, confused. "I, I didn't know."

"Shit," said the kid. "I could write a whole book about what you don't know."

TWELVE

Back in the reign of Woden, the *Council of Power* was kept more polished and plush, full of ornamental flourishes, silk veils strewn up on the ancient stone walls, abundant colors brought in to distract from the cold rock beneath. By order of the President, the fortress palace was maintained in a palatial state.

Dragomir had no use for such decoration. Dominion over the rising and ever-more powerful multitudes of armed humans is what concerned him.

At the periodic Supernatural gathering, an affair held each couple of years, all of the earth's Supers attended. So many faces and forms populated the *Great*

Hall that the collection was said to alter the gravitational field and weather patterns across continents. Human satellites performed erratically, and the magnetic shield, which surrounded the planet, tilted off its axis. Such enormous density of dark matter and energy squeezed within that single chamber could only be hypothesized by human scientists as some unexplainable solar-flare activity. It was the limit of their science.

President Woden spoke at the podium above them, his one damaged eye hidden beneath a black leather patch. He was flanked on one side by a pair of grey wolves, and on the other by his team of administrative subordinates. That clique was comprised of Dragomir, Pandora, Barby the Barbarian, Mr. Nukeman, Stellar, Quakestorm, and Shifty. These sat quietly together in an elevated section at the side of the carved stone stage. They listened respectfully to the *Council* President.

Woden's two black crows perched atop the jutting granite podium before him. These peered out across the sea of mutations below. His wolves similarly kept a paranoid vigilance. Woden's silver spear, Gungnir, rested beside him at his right hand.

"We seek not riches," said Woden, "nor domination over the humans. That must be clarion clear, and I will not speak further to this point." Woden's aging body was muscular and grey, and his voice bellowed commands. "We are, after all, of, by, and for another realm. What need have we to intervene in the affairs of humans?"

His gloved hand snatched up his spear, and he stormed past his wolves out of the *Great Hall* alone.

Dragomir's squinting yellow eyes scrutinized the reactions of the gathered Supernatural crowd. Most were difficult to read, enigmas that swiftly returned to invisibleness.

Woden's crows and his wolves trailed dutifully out after their lord. Dragomir and his group remained silent and still, off to the side of the stage, as the earth's Supernaturals dispersed back out into the world as swiftly as they had arrived.

When the *Great Hall* had cleared, Stellar spoke up, "I could snatch that spear right off his back before he had any idea what was happening."

Dragomir and Pandora froze simultaneously.

Dragomir murmured, "Watch your tongue, fool. He hears all."

Pandora bobbed her head. "He would smash you into a billion fragments, lightweight."

"No way," said the quick one, Stellar, drunk on his own arrogance.

Pandora emitted a pulsing green. "Don't you think he's considered such a ploy ten-thousand times before? And yet he's still here."

Stellar darted around them in a square.

Dragomir yawned. "You have moves, but lack mass. You are light as the air."

Pandora concurred. "Don't do anything stupid."

She stepped toward Stellar, her eyes pouring out white heat onto his soul. He seized in place, as she stepped up to his face, her index finger extended. Upon her touch, Stellar relaxed into a sleeping stare.

Dragomir looked on them with amusement.

"When we need you," said Pandora, "we'll let you know."

Stellar groggily nodded acquiescence.

The Barbarian clomped onto the stone floor behind them all. "New war in Africa! Who's coming?"

Dragomir rolled his eyes. "Enjoy yourself, my friend."

THIRTEEN

D'Andre Walker was flying and strapped onto Steve Arkin's back. Over the east river, over the skyscrapers, it was a quick trip, but his whole body went weak and shook. Trapped between the sun and the hard city landscape below, this was almost too much for him. His hands kept jittering.

Steve dropped right down in the middle of the amusement park. Coney Island was full up with people.

Passersby clicked cell phone photos, as D'Andre climbed down to the old wooden planks. Eventually, the spectators shuffled on and left them alone.

D'Andre sat on a bench to recover his strength.

Steve went over and bought a cotton candy.

D'Andre ate the treat while studying the surrounding ride options.

Super Steve pointed. "The *Tilt a Whirl* is a classic."

"I'll think about it."

The two strolled to sit at a nearby table. D'Andre relaxed again to catch his breath. It wasn't such a great day for this, but he didn't know if he was only getting worse anyway.

"You look more like you'd be into bumper cars," said Steve. "I used to love the bumper cars."

D'Andre observed some little kids scurrying along the boardwalk, followed by a man and woman pushing a baby stroller. He considered the other rides around him, and he inspected the front of the haunted house. He couldn't help but notice the faraway look on Super Steve's face.

"Steve?" said D'Andre. "What happened your family?"

Steve turned. "It was a car crash. My son, Michael, was five and a half."

D'Andre stared back. "He dead?"

"…Yeah."

"How the car crash?"

Steve jolted and turned away. "Just one of those things."

"Was you the driver?"

"Me? No. Hey, there's the bumper cars. I told you. Come on, buddy." Steve called with his hand, stepping away from him.

"Aiight." D'Andre climbed back to his feet and assessed the long walk to the flashing lights.

Nighttime fell. Neon lights spun. D'Andre had celebrated life enough. Super Steve flew him back across the river. Covertly, they snuck in through his room's unlocked window.

Steve helped him down to the floor. "Here you go. Had a good time?"

"Oh yeah. Thanks, Steve." D'Andre climbed back up to sit on his hospital bed.

Steve turned around. "Now, I've got to go."

D'Andre grabbed his wrist firmly. "Steve? Wait. Who was drivin' the car? What happened?"

Steve pried himself loose. Head low, he shuffled to the window and floated outside again. In the hazy orange glow of the street lamps below, he twisted back.

"My wife, Cathy."

D'Andre perked up in bed. "Did she die too?"

Steve shrugged. "She couldn't see where she was going, I guess."

"How come you didn't drive?"

"I had a few drinks. It was a party. All day long."

"Was she drunk?"

"No! I didn't say that. I. I had a few drinks that night."

"They all died? Everybody but you?"

"It's one of those things. It's nobody's fault."

Steve streaked off into the hazy grey.

FOURTEEN

Steve Arkin swiftly descended upon a brick tenement building on the north end of Manhattan. He set down on a balcony. Peeking inside, the room was a disheveled mess, objects smashed and thrown everywhere. The glass balcony door had shattered.

He cautiously entered and flicked on a light to search through an overturned pile of video production equipment. A photo on a bookshelf showed that journalist, Rick Jenkins, alongside some African villagers. Steve raised it to examine.

From room to room, the apartment was left

ransacked.

Steve felt his anger rise.

Memories flooded back from nowhere.

From the living room, Cathy screamed out, "Oww! Steve!"

He ran inside, looking around frantically. "What? What?"

Cathy held her hand over her eye, jumping about. "He hit me in the eye this time. Deal with him!" She rushed off to the bathroom, leaving him staring down on the two-year-old menace.

"Michael! What did you do?"

"No!" Michael raced off toward the playroom. Steve pursued and grabbed an arm.

Cathy shouted over the sound of running water, "Put him in the corner in time-out!"

He lifted Michael up and sat the little squirmer in the chair in the corner of the toy-strewn playroom. "You stay!"

"No!" The boy wiggled to escape.

Steve grabbed him by the shoulders and held him fast.

Michael wrestled crazily. "No! No!"

"Stop it!" Steve loomed over the toddler, unsure

how to communicate. The red-faced tantrum resisted normal methods of speech.

"Why did you hurt your mommy?"

"No!" The boy lunged to the side to get away.

Steve threw him back down into the corner. "Stop it!"

Staring down on Michael, he bored into the little blue eyes, searching for a spark of recognition, but he found none. It was as if there was no there there, no conscience, no responsibility, just a little monkey menace.

"Why! Did! You! Hurt! Your! Mommy?"

Michael rocked back and forth, trying to wrestle out of his grip.

Steve refused to fail. *What was inside this kid? He must have some primitive understanding. There must be something.*

"Listen to me."

"No!"

"You're gonna listen to me."

"No!"

"You little! You're not going anywhere until you listen."

"No! No!"

"No! I say no. I'm telling you no!"

"No!"

"No, I tell you no!"

"No no no no." Michael jerked repeatedly, still indignant.

Steve called back over his shoulder, "How do people keep from killing their kids?"

"Don't even say that!" Cathy appeared in the doorway, a washcloth covering her right eye. "Never say that, Steve. What's the matter with you?"

"What? He can't understand."

Michael bolted again, and Steve pushed him back. "No you don't."

"No, no, no, no!"

"Why the hell do people have children again?"

Behind him she scoffed, "Because you like the booty."

Steve nodded his head.

Cathy stepped forward. "Let me try... Michael?"

Steve backed away, flustered, his head reeling.

Cathy became sad and frail. "You made mommy cry. You hit mommy in the eye. Now mommy's gonna go cry."

Suddenly, the kid's attitude changed completely.

"Mommy?"

"Mommy sad. You hit mommy." Her acting convinced the little terror. Michael appeared sad with concern. He put his arms around Cathy's legs and squeezed.

"Don't make mommy sad."

"Yeah," said Steve. "Don't hit your mother. No!"

"You no," said the brat.

FIFTEEN

An alert squealed from a tiny speaker. President Dragomir glanced over at the security system. It was Steven Arkin, the human, and he had returned not so unexpectedly. Dragomir considered for an instant and then pressed the button. A minute later, Arkin stormed into his office in an expressly agitated state.

Dragomir listened quietly, as Arkin pressed his case again.

"This Rick Jenkins evidence is solid. The two are caught on the video. They killed the man and the baby."

"Tragic," said Dragomir. "Barbaric. No pun

intended. Drink?" He rose to saunter back to his bar and tinker with bottles in search of the right combination of sustenance and distraction.

Arkin vented behind him, "Mr. Nukeman and Mr. Barby must be held accountable. We have to do this for the sake of all of our legitimacy."

"They will be," said Dragomir. "Be assured." His finger pressed at the blender. He splashed in more alcohol and raw meat.

"How?" Arkin persisted. "A trial?"

"Oh, no no no. We won't air our dirty laundry for the human press to feast upon." He sipped at his breakfast concoction. "I will take care of this personally."

Arkin reclined back in the chair, across the desk, seemingly appeased for the moment. "What will you do?"

Dragomir reclaimed his throne across the stone desk.

"This will never happen again, Mr. Arkin. Thanks for coming by." He pressed a button, and the stone security door rumbled open behind Arkin's chair.

His fingernail gestured to make use of the portal.

Arkin rose, but he meandered lackadaisically.

"Wait," he said. "This is already public. You know we have to come clean to the humans."

"Nonsense!" Dragomir raised his voice. "This needs to go away. It's history. Don't rehash the past. I prefer to look forward. We can't bring back the dead, Mr. Arkin. You know that better than most."

Arkin's voice pleaded, in that cloying, repetitive, human manner that Dragomir so despised.

"If we don't show humanity that we value justice —"

Dragomir jolted, and he made use of his roaring timbre, "THEY'VE ALREADY FORGOTTEN THIS! The world moved on! You should too."

Arkin finally retreated to the doorway. "But, as the *Council of Power*, we have a duty—"

"Arkin," Dragomir sneered. "Our duty, *your* duty is to remain on good terms with the human infestation. And those are my direct instructions."

"That's—"

"There are eight billion of them! Armed to their monkey brains with hydrogen bombs. It is forgotten. All is well. Relax. Resume your smiling public photo opportunities with your children. Enjoy."

Arkin shook his head. "Not completely forgotten.

That journalist, Rick Jenkins, is now missing."

"Oh?"

Arkin cocked his head in that infuriating accusatory tic. "Any idea where he is?"

Dragomir ignored the piercing primate glance. "The moment I hear something, you'll be first on my list to contact. Thanks again for stopping in, *Lab Rat*."

Arkin gritted his teeth as he nodded. Without further fuss he departed the Presidential suite.

Dragomir sealed the stone chamber door with a gentle touch of another electronic button. Rumbling mechanisms crunched into place and echoed throughout the cavernous fortress. He watched Arkin fly off again on a video monitor, and he returned to the business at hand.

On his large wall screen icy tundra appeared.

"Done?"

Mr. Nukeman stepped into view. "Nobody's gonna look up here."

Off screen, the Barbarian chuckled.

Dragomir nodded.

Nukeman tilted his camera down at the hole in the ice, where the water quickly refroze. Flakes of snow settled into the black water. Beneath the surface lay a dark human form, a motionless Rick Jenkins, disposed of permanently.

When the humans first ripped the land asunder, erecting their monuments, their thick walls and cities, farming every square inch along the riverbank, it soon caught the attention of Dragomir, who had never given them a second thought before. Their intensive encroachment sickened him, upsetting the natural order of things and fouling his landscape more every day. Their cascading offenses erupted in his thoughts and gave him such disgust and a craving to roll back their development. It was three-thousand six-hundred odd years past, but the lessons of that time remained always within him.

After studying the arising human empire, its structures and, crucially, its leaders, Dragomir arrived at the doorstep of a provincial governor. When the pathetic little fat man emerged from his house entrance, Dragomir tore him apart at the limbs. He quickly devoured chunks of the man in front of his cowering family. Grasping a fractured arm bone, he scrawled symbols onto the official's white marble floor with his own excess blood. The first symbol designated the Emperor Shang. The second pictogram suggested that the dragon would be replacing him. It seemed a straightforward command, one even these insignificant inferiors might comprehend straight away.

Learning bits of their language and terrorizing groups of inhabitants at random, in a bid to subjugate the population, Dragomir soon entered into negotiations with Emperor Shang. His human legions instantly set to work constructing a tall towering palace fit for a dragon to gaze out over his subjects and remind them of their places far below. This pleased Dragomir, their total acquiescence and reverence for his superiority.

Human envoys promised him all the riches and slaves he might require. Dragomir gladly accepted their unconditional surrender. It was the pinnacle of his prestige. He would rule over every living thing in his dominion.

On one bright spring day, Dragomir flew over their primitive stone city surveying his kingdom. The humans scurried to race indoors in order to conceal themselves from his gaze. This was preferred, as the sight of them, like insects gathered, did tend to perturb him. Soon enough, Dragomir arrived at his newly-erected tower palace. Many colorful silks adorned the superstructure, typical human frivolousness. From his high perch above the empire, Dragomir would receive the emperor's jade *Seal of the Mandate of Heaven and Earth*. This symbolic ceremony was to alert their entire species that sovereignty had transferred onto him. It would be the Age of the Dragon, and this was an exercise of political authority.

When Dragomir arrived in the tower and he flew into the palace through an open wall overlooking the city of Shang-ti, the little emperor stood silently at a podium holding the jade seal and prepared for the transfer of power. Wearing formal yellow silk, the elderly little human stood motionless before his superior.

Dragomir touched down with all intention of humiliating his counterpart and tearing off his head simply to intimidate the rest. It was best not to leave one's competitors alive. They would only scheme tirelessly in the shadows. This much he had absorbed from his years of observing their own practices.

As Dragomir stepped forward to collect his prize, Emperor Shang pulled up on the jade seal with both his hands. Somehow this jerking action triggered a chain-reaction in the building's architecture. Dragomir instantly found the overhead rafters had been weighed down heavily. The ceiling caved in upon him. The floor collapsed beneath in a near total demolition.

Shang remained perched on a solid ledge of stone, while Dragomir plummeted story after story into a gaping hole beneath the massive hollow tower. Stone pillars, bags weighted down with rocks, bronze-tipped spears protruding from the basement floor, many tons of debris flattened him at the bottom of the collapse.

Dragomir soon learned that he was immobile and trapped helplessly beneath the human rubble pile. All his strength and ferocity useless when compacted into the earth's crust like an beetle smashed across a stone. He had never before conceived it possible to be defeated by his lessors.

All his supernatural might struggled to extricate himself, but it was ineffective. Dragomir lay beneath the ground, another ancient fossil to be extricated in some unknown distant millennium. Lost, without hope of escape, he settled in as an earth spirit. Forever, he contemplated the human menace, which he had so mistakenly underestimated. Its deceptiveness and its collective engineering prowess, these were hidden muscles. Although single humans might easily be dismembered, the horde and its technological mastery of warfare could prove resilient, to say the least.

Dragomir's blinding hot rage passed on to cold calculation as he endured his centuries beneath the rocks and dirt.

SIXTEEN

Steve returned to the big city that night and headed in toward that familiar silver skyscraper, slowly closing in on the array of enticing windows stretched across the luminous penthouse suite. Silently, he lingered, hovering close enough to spy down into the loft below. There he held, unsure about the situation's etiquette.

His fingers gently tapped on the glass.

As he did, Pandora, Miss Melt, strolled into view below, glowing in peach tones. But she seemed oblivious to his presence and glided around her trees and flowers to the open space at the couches. Stopped there, she untied her silver dress.

Steve stared down entranced, as her skin emitted soft golden rays, and she kicked off her dainty silver shoes.

Pandora floated several inches, wearing nothing but her *Victoria's Secrets* and sailed around a corner and out of sight. She was gone.

Steve held fast outside her window, waiting for some indication from her. None came.

From the rooftop above, a water-balloon smashed onto his head.

"Ahh! What?"

Pandora's bounding, ethereal voice giggled, somewhere above on the roof.

Steve jolted to his senses, and he rose to the top edge to peek over. Built into her roof sat a massive blue swimming pool illuminating the deck with dancing waves. He couldn't locate Miss Melt anywhere, and so he gently slid higher. Onto the concrete, and he strolled toward the pool. Now self-conscious, his fingers combed his wet hair back into place.

Looking down into the pool at the water's edge, but Pandora jetted up from below the surface and grabbed him like a Mermaid, yanking him right into the pool with her.

He and she twisted in the bubbles. She glowed pink with delight. Her face illuminated the night. Steve was mesmerized by her, as they tumbled in circles.

Face to face, she blinded him with energies. Her hair fanned out beneath the water and flared with sparks in the escaping bubbles. They moiled over and over until Steve's mind was reduced to dizzy stupefaction.

Flipping orientation with Pandora, within her flaring rainbow aura and black bubbles, she attacked him with her lips. Her arms grappled hard as she spun him in endless spirals beneath the water. Twirling together as one, Steve felt his brain melt away gazing into her hypnotic bright eyes.

As Miss Melt pulled him in for another kiss, he had no knowledge of relocating. They hovered above her bed, still rotating randomly as if underwater. He could sense nothing beyond the flood of her energy fields, which she had enveloped him in.

Time evaporated.

Steve knew only that she controlled him fully. There could be no reason to fight her. She was too angelic to doubt. He wanted only to possess her face to the fullest, but now it had become multi-layered.

Pandora was happy, intense, commanding, pliant, all simultaneously as if she had multiplied across overlapping dimensions. There was another version of her each moment.

Steve pondered his cursory knowledge of quantum concepts, bridging universes, doorways to multiple realms. But it was too complicated to dwell on for more than half a second. His perceptions dissolved one after the other, melted away. This was how she had become known as Miss Melt. There was nothing to think or feel except Pandora. Everything was Pandora. So many versions of her danced about him, as they slammed together as one.

Steve began to notice more than one iteration of himself as well, replications. Unsure which entity was the true one, he lost all perspective on reality in her unceasing deluge of pleasures.

SEVENTEEN

President Woden barked "No!" He whipped about to storm away from them.

Dragomir bowed subserviently.

Miss Melt spied on at the two from the dim shadows of the stone fortress corridor. While Dragomir stood stoically, Woden stomped forward on the cobblestones. Woden always carried Gungnir strapped across his back. Flanked by his contingent of wolves and crows, the President approached her hiding spot.

Pandora stepped out and dared to block his path. "Mr. President?"

The elder Woden froze in a stunned moment, his

good eye adjusting to her soft pulsing radiance.

"Pandora."

She smiled at him and gazed innocently up.

Woden's beasts monitored her with cold caution.

In her penthouse loft, Pandora sprayed mist onto her jungle flowers. A trio of spider monkeys swung about on branches at the ceiling.

"He can see the future," she said. Her fingers caressed the delicate yellow petals, imbuing them with her white energy.

"Nonsense," argued Dragomir, behind her. "He has erred."

"When?"

"I saw it. With both my eyes. He lacks perfect knowledge."

"He'll see this coming," she said, and she twisted to point an admonishing finger at her unruly Lynx, who was set to pounce. The cat purred knowingly.

"I think not," argued the half-dragon. "He is quite blinded by the likes of you. Or didn't you know?"

"I know." She rolled her eyes and continued misting her jungle garden.

Dragomir floated around the front to face her. "Fill his single eye with the ecstasy he craves most dearly."

In the stone palace corridor, Pandora sensed that she had attracted Woden, but he maneuvered around her anyway to continue his official business. At the President's suite, at the far end of the hallway, its massive stone door unlatched for him to reenter his chamber.

But before his door had shut her out, Pandora followed him inside.

Woden whipped back toward her. "Pandora? Yes?"

She brightened yellow, her hair crackling at the ends, blue sparks and bright yellow skin. "Mr. President, if I can just have a minute?"

The tall stone doors latched automatically behind her.

Woden removed the spear from his back, and he rested it in a rack above his desk chair.

"Very well," he said. "Sit with me."

As Pandora slowly settled into her seat across the stone desk, Woden stared on across at her. His wolves yawned and his crows came to rest about the room.

Pandora sized up the elder male demigod. "I'd just like to have a more vital role to play," she said. "I'd like to be closer to you, if you don't mind me hanging about."

"Of course not," said Woden, almost smiling. "I have always appreciated you."

"I wouldn't dare to get in your way, or to annoy you, Woden."

He sat back, his wrinkly grey face pliant like a ventriloquist's doll.

Pandora cooled her energy to soften her radiance toward a more natural, almost human spectrum.

EIGHTEEN

Steve Arkin awoke from smacking kicks at the back of his bare thighs. "What? What?"

Golden sun blazed in through Pandora's array of windows stretched above them.

He twisted his body over, wrapped within her silken sheets. He was naked, and she continued to poke her foot at him

Pandora was sat at the foot of the bed, temperamentally filing her nails. "You have to go, Steve."

"What's the hurry?"

"I've been sitting here for hours!"

He shrugged. "D-Don't you sleep?"

"Why the hell would I sleep? Do you know who I am?"

He froze. "No. Not really."

Pandora sprang up impatiently, blowing on her fingernails. She seemed to directly absorb the sun's rays bending them toward her in the brutal glare of the city's morning. "Come on. Get dressed."

"Okay. Okay. I'm going." Steve scurried to locate his socks and underwear. "Good morning by the way. I had a—"

"Yeah, I've got tons of work, and people to deal with. Let s get you movin' out." Her crackling, electrified fingers pushed his damp shirt into his arms, and she guided him awkwardly toward her doorway.

Steve slid on his pants, feeling like a misbehaved teenager. He found himself lost in her floral maze.

"Left turn, Steven."

"You sure do have a serious garden."

"I've always been anthophilous. It's well known."

A nasty-looking mid-sized wildcat snarled out at him from the leaves.

"Whoa." Behind him, another large cat jumped into position and bared its teeth. Its thin, pointy ears jutted up.

Pandora barked at them, "Ocelot. Lynx. No. Behave."

Steve spun left and right to find a third predator, a bobcat stalking him overhead on the branch of some exotic jungle tree.

"Aren't those all from different climates?"

Pandora prodded him through her rain forest toward the exit doors. "They adapt, Steven, when they have no choice."

"I see that. Any other wild creatures I should—"

"Just me."

"Yeah."

She guided him through her loft maze and to the double doors. "Let's go, let's go…"

When he finally hit the empty hallway, he rotated back in some confusion. "Did I do something?"

She stretched, hanging onto the jamb of the door. "Not really."

Steve shrugged. "I don't get it."

Her energy fluctuated at a low flicker, shades of violet and pink. "Look, Steven, you're really cute and all, but I just thought it would be a bit more… super."

Steve flushed red. "Oh. I had a really long day

yesterday. I mean brutal."

She giggled. "Not long enough. Ha ha ha…"

Steve froze in horror.

Pandora slammed the doors in his face. "I'll call you sometime."

Steve slid on his damp shirt, and he found only one sock, but both his shoes. Finger pressed the silver elevator button, which dinged immediately. He bounced on one foot, balancing awkwardly to work his final shoe on.

Inside the elevator, Quakestorm charged out. A massive Supernatural so powerful he exuded energy and a low-frequency rumble everywhere he went. His skin looked like a patchwork of dark river stones. Fields vibrated intensely in concentric waves away from him, and the lights flickered as he passed them.

Steve nearly fell into Quakestorm, who shot out like a steamroller. He flew back across the hallway.

"Idiot." Quakestorm glared back, with black primordial eyes and then stomped up to Miss Melt's door.

Steve stood watching from the elevator, and he attempted to assess the cacophony of strange energies bleeding out from that weird ancient thing in front of him. His nose smelled the radiation, and his skin felt the pulsing waves lapping at him like the ocean.

Just before the doors slid closed, Steve saw Quakestorm enter a code into the security keypad on the wall and let himself into Pandora's penthouse suite.

Steve's confidence deflated as the elevator plummeted swiftly toward ground.

NINETEEN

Claude LaGrange ignored the increasing mound of newspapers piled up on his doorstep. Something about the Supernatural "Quakestorm" held zero interest, partly because he was not invited to the Pentagon's little party, whatever it was. Many miles from the Nevada test range, all the hyped-up warnings seemed overstated, that monotonous hysteria from the press concerning all things supernatural. They feared what they lacked the capacity to understand. His remote Nevada town was perfectly safe.

LaGrange sustained his purely scientific explorations down in his basement laboratory. His small particle accelerator would be next to worthless without his newly discovered catalyst to entangle dark matter and to upend the known laws of the universe. Anyone could smash particles against one another, but to cause dark matter to stick around for human observation and manipulation required a distinct, unique recipe previously unknown.

The paperboy on his bicycle had demanded payment, but LaGrange had no patience for the ebb and flow of mundane commerce. A headline he shuffled past that day said, *NEVADA BRACES FOR SEISMIC TEST... HANG ON TO YOUR HATS, PARDNERS*. The front page, above the fold, featured photos of that Supernatural thing Quakestorm. It said that his cooperation with the U.S. Army would benefit the United States' military in some vague way. A hint of a new strategic advantage if the government partnered with the Supernaturals. It seemed like nothing so much as a photo opportunity, muscle flexing, more Cold War propaganda.

The real progress happened through meticulous measurement of quantum events. LaGrange raced inside his house to continue his quest for the elusive solution to one of the fundamental questions plaguing physics. As every astronomical calculation demanded, dark matter must exist in some form, but no human being had ever before touched it or attempted to control it. This time would be different. This modern Holy Grail, black gold, a resource so mysterious as to be monopolized by the one who cracked its code—a gold rush had launched where no human had ever before seen a single nugget.

LaGrange's sole test subject, the one on which so much relied, was the comatose Steven Arkin. For months Arkin lay on a cot aided and monitored by machines. Oxygen and nutrient tubes kept him alive. This Arkin had been undergone a series of clinical trials, but he remained unresponsive and vegetative. Perhaps he was just dead.

LaGrange's laboratory, just below ground level, held radioactive, biological and chemical hazards cooking around the concrete perimeter. In HazMat protective gear, he operated his particle-accelerator, while Bunsen burners and petri-dishes churned with automated computer guidance.

Those radio frequencies carrying the classical music he loved so dearly suddenly crackled with warning squeals. The military's test proceeded. *Project Martini*, a nice touch, 'shaken not stirred.' The young woman, some Lieutenant no doubt, echoed across the desert floor, "Ten, nine, eight, seven, six..."

LaGrange yawned, flicked his cigarette, and breathed in the smoke derisively. Returning to his electron-microscope, he said, "Blah, blah, blah."

"Three, two..."

LaGrange's particle accelerator whined at top speed, as did his generators. He adjusted his viewfinder and typed in a measurement. His multi-tasking overwhelmed, but he had no funds to hire an assistant.

When the shock wave hit with force enough to knock every item, every table, every shelf, and all of his machinery across to the far cinder block wall, it ignited a chain of events. The initial blast was followed by a barrage of x-rays and gamma rays. Multiple explosions blew the cellar apart, as the entire laboratory flared into a blinding white fireball.

Sparks danced randomly across the surfaces.

Some minutes later, Dr. LaGrange awoke and pulled himself from beneath the debris. He could see again through the caustic smoke, and he saw his catalyst splattered across the dirty concrete floor. Sparkling with radioactive annihilations, the black goo held a sheen insulating it from what appeared to be the earth's atmosphere. It lived in its own bubble, some miniaturized, gooey black hole, for which he had only educated guesses as to its atomic makeup, but he knew that any guesswork would be a lie. If it was real, if he wasn't hallucinating, this would be a turning point in the evolution of mankind.

LaGrange looked to his own hands where the skin had melted in patches. He body was burned and charred. Radiation flooded through him like a broken dam. Quickly, he snatched an unbroken beaker and a flat paper card to scrape up the black catalyst. Crawling as he choked on the fumes, he hunted down every minuscule drop of that otherworldly specimen.

TWENTY

D'Andre Walker curled up on the tray table. A hundred and four degrees out today, and the air conditioning was broken again. His guts on fire, everything ached so hard he couldn't straighten his body out inside the CAT scanner contraption like the nurses wanted him to.

Nurse Shondra bugged him over a speaker, even though he couldn't breathe 'cause of the heat and the pain. The meds had his muscles feeling all twisted up inside, and he couldn't get enough air. Now he was scared, and he jumped around to try and slide back out of the clanging monster that was trying to eat him alive.

"I can't do it!"

Nurse Shondra talked in a microphone, louder than the death robot.

"You can't move, D'Andre. Stay still, or we gotta do it again."

"I can't! I can't!"

The clanking rapid-fire bursts rattled his nerves, pounded his skull and his belly, his chest, and everywhere.

He was gonna die. His eyes started to go black, and he cried.

Then the evil machine went quiet. D'Andre opened his eyes again. Behind him, Supernatural Steve appeared. The CAT scan table slid back out with its motors.

D'Andre realized he had tears ran down his face. He wiped quickly with his sleeve.

"Hey little man," said Steve.

"Hey."

"I think you're all done." Steve pulled a wheelchair around, beside the sliding table.

"Yeah," said Nurse Shondra. "It's all over baby. Go get some breakfast. Good job, D'Andre."

He plopped down hard, and his head flailed back weakly.

"Are you hungry?" asked Super Steve.

"I don't know."

Steve pushed him in his chair around and out of the lab, into the hospital's hallway. Steadily they rolled toward the cafeteria.

D'Andre didn't feel hungry.

Steve said, "What are you hungry for, man?"

"I don't know. Pancakes."

They pivoted around the corner, and the cafeteria entrance rolled into view with the smell of frying eggs and bacon.

Steve said, "They have 'em in there?"

D'Andre shrugged. "Yeah. But they ain't no good."

"Huh." Steve stopped pushing the wheel chair.

D'Andre twisted back over his shoulder.

Steve pointed backward. "What about that pancake house down the street?"

D'Andre perked up. "Oh no. They're good. My grandpops used to take me there sometimes."

"Well, let's go there."

"Do it."

Steve wheeled them around and headed for the exit.

The sun blinded D'Andre, who hadn't brought his sunglasses. He covered his eyes, as they rolled toward the restaurant.

"Nice day," said Steve.

"Eh."

"Well it's gonna get better. Trust me."

Straight up the ramp and into the *Pancake Hut*, D'Andre could smell the fresh batter frying in butter on the skillet, maple syrup and whipped cream shot out of a can. It was just what he needed. "I love this place. Now I'm hungry!"

D'Andre found himself rolled next to a booth, and he climbed over to slide onto the bench. "Now this is more like it! That hospital stuff gets on my last nerve. I can't handle it, man. I like good food."

Steve nodded.

A waitress stepped over with a pad and pen. A young local girl about twenty, her face flashed with shock. "Oh my God! You're Super Steve!"

Steve smiled, and pointed right back at D'Andre. "Well he's super too."

"For reals?" The girl danced back in stunned confusion and bent down in D'Andre's face to get a good look. "You a supernatural?"

Steve laughed. "As super as they come."

D'Andre felt embarrassed. "Nah. Not really."

"Oh my God," she repeated. "I gots to get a picture. This is too much! In my booth!"

D'Andre hacked his way through his stack of strawberry-covered pancakes, doused with syrup, topped with whipped cream. He felt much improved over this morning.

Steve sat across, just sipping his coffee, and asked, "So what did your doctor say?"

D'Andre wiped his mouth aggressively to catch all the stray syrup. "Nothin', that means nothin'."

"Was it the medical terms you didn't understand?"

D'Andre shook his head. "Nah. They don't want to tell me it's over."

"You don't know that for sure."

He placed down his fork. "I seen out in the hall, when the doc comes reads the chart. He got pain on his face, man. He don't wanna say."

Steve sat listening.

D'Andre guzzled down his hot chocolate. "Ah! Hot!" He blew on it, but his tongue had already burned.

Steve said, "You have any relatives that come in

and see ya?"

"My grandpops, sometimes. But he works a lot."

Steve exhaled with a pause. "About the, the other thing. I'm still not sure what's going to happen."

D'Andre shrugged. "It's okay."

"I went and saw Dragomir, in person. I told him to his face what was on that video."

"What he say?"

"He said he would handle it."

"When?"

Steve shrugged back. "He said it would never happen again."

D'Andre nodded, and he chomped down the very last bite of his pancake. "Til next time."

TWENTY ONE

Steve Arkin strolled out the main doors of the Bronx Children's Hospital alone. Feet rose a few inches from the sidewalk, but then he decided to set back down and just walk it.

The neighborhood seemed dismal, dirty, with broken bottles, abandoned car skeletons. Homeless men lay wedged in beneath rusted iron structures. Brick and billboards, traffic lines and angry honking horns.

As Steve rounded the corner toward the nearest bridge, the scene appeared to change. The brick-faced towers of Manhattan dwarfed all the little lives, and their problems were rendered inconsequential. But this was just an illusion. Nothing had truly changed, only a simple view, a matter of focus, perspective.

Steve jumped up onto the bridge walkway and

continued his stroll back across the placid grey river. There was an inherent unfairness to it all that gnawed at him, but he couldn't define it.

Dropping down again to a street at the waterfront, his eyes scanned the buildings. Neon signs flickered in the harsh daylight. Their call subconscious, he beelined to the nearest sports bar. Plunging into the darkness, he found workmen with their beers chattering and drowning their sorrows.

Steve never drank alcohol to forget, but the opposite. His memories prior to his extended coma were spotty and decimated. He wanted to feel the before, but it remained elusive behind a wall of what he assumed to be impenetrable dark matter, that catalyst encapsulating his cells.

He claimed a stool at the stained-wood bar, and he tossed a hundred-dollar bill in front of him. A baseball game played above on all the television screens.

The gruff, bearded bar man took a second look at his face but seemed not to place him.

Steve said, "I'll have whatever's on tap... And give me a shot. Scotch, something from the top shelf."

"You got it."

Steve nodded to approve the label, and he

guzzled down his whiskey. The bartender slid a cold frosty mug over.

He held up his shot glass. "Another one of these, please."

The bar man whipped about to retrieve the bottle.

Steve nursed his beer for some time.

His emotional memory kicked in, like he could recall something through his Swiss cheese brain. A wooden bat struck a baseball with a wicked crack. His head jolted to gaze up at the ballgame on the screen until it all blurred out.

Michael was five when he stood on the front lawn with a yellow plastic bat. A whiffle ball rested on a vertical orange tube beside him.

"All right Mikey. I'm gonna pitch it. When I say now, you swing."

"Okay."

Steve wound up and pretended to throw a ball. "All right, hit it!"

Michael swung and knocked the hollow ball back over Steve's head.

He turned in a circle, speechless. "Yes! Yes!" He ran and picked up Michael to spin him around. "You're gonna be good!"

Some wrinkled geezer stuck his face in closely. "Hey! You're Supernatural Steve Arkin!"

Steve snapped to reality in the crowded pub. He didn't know how many hours or how many drinks had passed through him, but he was still seated at that sports bar.

"Yeah, that's me."

The oldster wagged his index finger. "I knew it. I told 'em, and they didn't believe me."

A big burly workman shuffled up behind Steve's bar stool and announced, "Hia there *Lab Rat!* How's it goin?"

Steve jumped up from his stool, knocking it back over. He grit his teeth, jaw locked in anger. "I'd appreciate if you didn't call me that. To my face. In public." He slammed his glass beer mug onto the bar, and it shattered into a million pieces. Steve didn't flinch, eyes locked on the offending stranger.

The entire bar took an icy step back away from him.

He gazed all around at their faces. His brain was

impaired, but the anger was stronger.

They were afraid.

Steve rocked in place unsteadily, but he didn't care all that much about making a spectacle. He was used to it. His life was in the limelight now.

That burly man held his palms out in front of him. "I'm sorry Mr. Arkin. Let me get you a refill? Barman get Mr. Arkin another one please. Two! Yeah two. Whatever he wants."

Steve retrieved his stool from off the ground, and he sat back down. In silent frustration, he twisted himself back toward the televised ballgame. The pub's patrons, behind him, gravitated back toward some uneasy normality. He could feel their eyes on his back, and he knew he could never fit in here. He didn't fit in anywhere anymore.

At the payphone, in the wood-paneled hallway, Steve's shoulder gouged a dent into the wall accidentally. He dialed the phone.

"Yes?" said Miss Melt.

Her voice soothed and mesmerized him across the expanse.

"Guess who?"

"Huh," she said. "I don't remember giving you

this number."

"I had a question."

"Is it a stalkery kind of question?"

"Why does Quakestorm have a code to walk into your place?"

"Ha ha ha…"

"No. Really. It's s-slightly weird. Isn't it?"

She giggled with ethereal timbre. "You are splattered!"

"I just was looking out for you, is all."

"Well. The Quake could certainly rock my world, baby… if he didn't have a face like an orangutan's ass!"

"I just." Steve froze, and stood up tall. "How are you?"

"You do not do jealous well."

"Not jealous. Not. Just."

"What?"

"Nothing. You have a real good night." His finger clicked the lever to hang up. He strolled back across the bar, flipping through his wallet.

"Barkeep. Here. And take some more. Get everybody a round. Keep the change."

The excited proprietor snapped to. "You got it, Steve. Come back any time."

He nodded back, just about to exit into the night, when Pandora appeared again on all the TV screens in some prerecorded late news interview. Like a crashed computer, Steve's mind froze in front of the nearest screen, smiling uncontrollably at her oddly dancing sparkles.

Pandora said, "Interim President Dragomir intends to make a major address to world leaders at the United Nations on the twenty-fifth, at noon."

As *Council* spokesperson, Miss Melt made periodic announcements to the human media for them.

Steve felt confused. *An address to the humans about what?*

The slick, suited news anchor Brett bantered back, "The twenty-fifth of this month?"

"Correct," she said in her glowing otherworldliness. "We will formally notify the UN tomorrow of the *Council* President's intention to speak."

She and Brett occupied separate boxes on each side of the screen.

"I'm sure he'll be quite welcome, and we will all be curious as to his address."

"Thanks for having me, Brett."

Steve gazed as she looked directly back at him

through the screen. *Could she know he was watching? Would she even care?*

As he stepped out of the waterfront bar alone into the tenebrous Manhattan backstreets, Steve pondered this new announcement from the *Council of Power.*

TWENTY TWO

When the White House learned that the very first human-turned-Supernatural was an American, they immediately invited Steve in for a *Congressional Medal of Honor*. He was provided specific security instructions to avoid any potential mishaps with the Secret Service. Barred from restricted airspace, he met his security detail outside of the *Watergate Hotel*. There he entered a secure limousine and was driven off to visit the President.

It was Steve's first experience in the Oval Office. He strolled in flanked by nervous, black-suited men who wielded sub-machine guns and mumbled into their shoulders.

Cameras flashed, as he shook the President's hand. "Mister President, I wanted to say—"

"Hang on Mr. Arkin," said the Commander in Chief. "We've been unable to determine if you're a registered Democrat or a Republican!"

The entire office laughed out loud, as if it was obligatory.

"Oh," said Steve. "I'm independent, I suppose. I don't follow politics all that much."

Tossing back his head, the President said, "That's quite all right. No problem. The point is we're all good Americans."

"I suppose I am that."

"Well, excellent—"

"But sir," Steve interrupted. "I haven't actually done anything to merit this honor. I wouldn't feel right about accepting it. Wouldn't that diminish the medal for all those other recipients who sacrificed so much?"

"Oh, nonsense," said the President. "You're a Supernatural, and you're American. You are destined for great acts beyond what even our greatest heroes have accomplished. I'm certain of it. It's symbolic, Steve, and I feel in my heart," he touched his chest, "that you should accept it and remember it always as you move forward from here."

A spate of spontaneous applause broke out around the office.

Steve held fast for a moment. "Okay. Sir. If you think it's that important."

"It is, Mister Arkin. It most certainly is. That's why we're all here today. Just for this."

More cameras flashed.

The large, golden, five-starred medal was hung about Steve's neck on a blue ribbon, and he smiled purposefully beside the President through the photo session. The Vice President and the other representatives squeezed in for additional shots beside him.

After the room cleared out, Steve was left with only the President and a Secret Service detail. A small jewelry box came out. He assumed it was to store his new medal.

In a hushed voice, the President said, "This is for you too,"

Inside the blue velvet box sat a thick and expensive silver watch, little diamonds at three, six, nine and twelve o'clock.

"Oh wow." Steve felt taken aback.

The POTUS grinned. "This is no normal watch." He flipped it over and wrestled with the metal disc sealing the back. "If you can get it open." The President laughed. "There!"

When the cover was removed, he showed Steve the inner compartment. The mechanism had been miniaturized, leaving empty room within the small cavity.

"It's a spy watch, courtesy of the talented bastards deep within the intelligence community."

Steve examined the device. It seemed harmless enough.

"See there?" The President elbowed at him. "You can fit a flash card, or even a .22 bullet, if you need one."

"I won't be needing any bullets, sir."

"Ah. Well you never know. Point is it's yours. However you may choose to employ it."

Steve accepted the gift. "Thank you, again."

"We're just always here for you. America is behind you one hundred percent. We all want to be your backup, Steve."

"That's good to know."

The President whispered, "If you happen to come

across important information, from wherever. Other governments. Or the *Supernatural Council* for example?"

"I see." Steve popped the rear disc back onto the watch, and he returned it to its case.

Still inebriated from the night's consumption at the bar, Steve landed on the balcony where yellow police tape and a cloudy sheet of plastic blocked the hole. He ripped a tear, and he entered Rick Jenkins' dark, empty apartment.

Fingerprint dust coated much of the place and remained on an 8x10" photograph of Jenkins. Steve snatched the picture and flew off with it out and up through the cloud layers, through the upper elevations toward space.

Sunrise approached on the curved edge of the globe.

He shot off over the ocean along the airless border of black and blue. There he felt a directional pull, navigation through the dark matter fields. A gut feeling gnawed inside, his internal compass. Steve's autopilot was subconscious, drawn from all the dark energy fields splashing about from the motions of other Supers. He could almost sense the many disturbances below on the planet's surface from all of the Supernatural activities.

Putrid black smoke rose high above a burning battlefield.

Steve caught sight of a flare, a bright yellow radiation beam. As he descended to the earth, he surveyed the full horror of the charred plain, corpses and burnt vehicles overturned, crackling flames in the dry grass. Bomb craters scarred the landscape for miles.

Africa was known to be hot with perpetual wars, but Steve had never visited before.

One tall grey smoke plume differed from the others. Barby the Barbarian cooked himself breakfast over a makeshift barbecue.

Steve set down quietly and strolled toward the giant.

On a lounge chair beside the gargantuan, Mr. Nukeman peered out through binoculars and blasted beams through he lenses into the treeline.

Screams echoed off in the distance, interspersed with bursts of automatic gunfire from Aks, plus the occasional explosion.

The Barbarian called over his shoulder. "Ours? Or theirs?"

Nukeman shrugged indifferently. He lay back to soak up the sun with his bare chest.

The Supernatural pair remained uninterested in Steve as he crept up to their makeshift fire pit.

Barby lifted a leg from the flames, and his teeth ripped off a chunk of thigh meat. It was human.

"It's my own barbecue sauce. It's tasty. You should try."

Nukeman turned up his nose, completely ignoring Steve's presence. "What's in it?"

Barby huffed. "Secret."

Steve suppressed his better judgment and pushed in between the two of them. "I'm looking for Rick Jenkins."

Barby and Nukeman grinned with caustic amusement.

The radioactive one said, "Who?"

Steve held up the photograph of Jenkins. Its shadow fell across Nukeman's face. He pushed the picture down. "The journalist who put your faces up on the Internet."

Nukeman's hellish yellow eyes glowed subtly in the hot African sun. "Why would we know?"

Behind Steve the Barbarian chuckled with

malicious delight.

Steve stood between the two, attempting to watch them both.

Nukeman dug into his own plate of meat, clicking his tongue as he chewed. "I heard he went skiing."

Barby laughed hard. "Ice skating."

"Yeah, Lab Rat. He had a beautiful triple Axel."

Steve stepped back from the barbecued human feast.

"Had?"

Nukeman barked, "Yeah. Had. Has. What's it to you? You're startin' to get on our nerves, Lab Rat."

Arkin took up a position where he could monitor them both, the three of them in a tight triangle. He said, "Jenkins' video never made it to prime time TV. I'm not sure how you arranged that."

Nukeman shrugged. "So?"

Steve grinned.

"Well. Thing is, they still love having me up on all the networks. It's like an open door policy."

The Barbarian dropped his breakfast back down onto the grill. "What are you saying?"

"You've got twenty-four hours to produce Rick

Jenkins."

Nukeman stood up clumsily from his cot, and the three circled around each other. "Or what?"

The Barbarian held up his massive palms in disbelief. "You threatening us?"

Steve coldly eyed them both.

Nukeman snickered. "Now you've gone and screwed with Barby's breakfast time, Rat. Not smart."

The Barbarian pointed a massive finger. "You cry when you step on an ant, Rat Boy?"

Steve retreated another step. "You bring me Jenkins, or I'm going public. In case you haven't heard, the public just adores me. Not sure how they feel about you two, since that South American thing."

Nukeman shook his head and scowled. "That ain't the way it's gonna go."

"You doubt me?"

"Sorry, Lab Rat. You just made the list." Radiation blasted from Nukeman's eyes.

Steve leapt straight up out of the way.

The beam accidentally burned Barby's arm, as he lunged to grab at Steve's feet.

"Ow!!! What the hell, Nuke? Watch it!"

The two rocketed up into the sky behind him. As

Steve raced up toward the puffy clouds, he changed his mind. Instead, he dove at a burning tank abandoned on the battlefield. Grabbed it by its turret, he spun it like a cyclone. Steve heaved the tank at Nukeman, who tried to melt it in the air, but failed. The molten machine bashed Nukeman sideways.

"AHHHH!"

Barby pursued across the battlefield toward the next wreckage pile. "You want to play!"

He came in fast like a bull in a China shop. Grabbing burnt jeeps and artillery pieces, Barby hurled them one after the other at Steve.

Steve dodged the flying armaments.

Nukeman's beam scorched Steve's chest and sent him tumbling back with a flaming hole in his shirt. His chest was burned red.

He rocketed up into the blue. They pursued him.

He tried to hide in a cloud layer, camouflaging his retreat. Below, he located the Atlantic coast.

Despite the fog, Nukeman and Barby gained on him. The clouds thinned out, and they had him.

Steve suddenly dove under the ocean. Below the surface he dropped as quickly as possible into the dark depths.

Barby and Nukeman splashed in behind him.

Steve dove for the bottom until the ocean light turned to darkness.

At another section of the coast, Steve rocketed up out of the saltwater, like a missile shot back into the clouds.

TWENTY THREE

Along dreary New York night, D'Andre Walker fidgeted in his hospital bed. His automatic blood-pressure monitor inflated and deflated softly on his biceps. He felt bed sore, spending most of his days lying around waiting for it to be over.

Flapping shadows flickered in the orange halogen lights outside his sixth-floor window. Massive wings spread in the moonlight.

Dragomir himself climbed in through the window and entered the tiny hospital room.

It seemed like a numb nightmare, just a faraway dream. D'Andre tried to open his drugged eyes, but it didn't seem real enough to bother about anyway.

Dragomir stepped up to the light switch and flicked it on, changing everything.

D'Andre flickered to consciousness.

Dragomir's glowing red eyes peered down on him. His clawed reptilian finger tapped on his forehead.

"Aaaaa! Aaaaa!" D'Andre jolted and squirmed away to the far edge of his little bed. His blood pressure spiked to 150/90.

"Shhh!" Dragomir stood tall like a vampire. "Silence, young man."

D'Andre shifted his body upward against his pillow, shivering.

The half-dragon beamed down on him with those beady eyes. The silver spear across his back scraped a line in the ceiling tiles.

D'Andre stared up, immobile.

Dragomir checked out in the hallway, through the door's glass, and he whipped back. "What were you thinking?"

D'Andre's hand hunted for the emergency call button on the bedside rail.

"You're having a new dream," said Dragomir, "and a new *wish* to tell Mr. Arkin immediately."

D'Andre gawked up in silence. His blood pressure

spiked again 180/115. He could feel his body losing control, but he couldn't do anything to stop it. His hands shook, and he breathed harder. His stomach throbbed, and he thought he might wet the bed.

Dragomir gazed off. "Your new wish is for the Supernaturals to all coexist peacefully." He spread his leathery arms for effect. "And to forget the past. Look to a bright sunny future. Do you understand me? Master Walker?"

D'Andre nodded. "Mmm. You killed Woden."

Dragomir grunted, caught off guard. "And what was so special about the old Norse tyrant?"

"It was a age a inspiration." D'Andre shivered.

"Well, then perhaps I felt inspired. Consider that I merely assisted the old anachronism off to find a better place."

"But—"

"Silence! Ignorant cub. Woden the Berserker was the most feared and unstable dictator the earth had ever known, for thousands of blood-washed years. I saved you all from the whimsical ravings of that old lunatic. Have you no concept of the numbers of your kind that Woden lay waste over the millennia?"

The beeping heart monitor sped faster. D'Andre

tingled with uncertainty. "You're a liar."

"I suppose I am to take insult?" Dragomir droned on icily. "End your suffering quickly? Hmm. You would be not even an inconsequential morsel for one of Woden's ravenous pets. Nothing more."

D'Andre leaned back dizzily into his pillow, blood pressure soaring out of control.

Dragomir bent in close toward his face. "Call off your rat, or some very, very disagreeable things will transpire."

Blood pressure rose to 204/127. D'Andre grabbed his chest, heaving and gasping.

Dragomir's claw reached out and petted D'Andre on his bald head.

"Good."

Room rolling, D'Andre lunged for the hanging switch box and pressed the shining red emergency button. Tiny red flashes shot out as his mind expired.

TWENTY FOUR

Steve Arkin rushed into the emergency room and to the front desk at the Bronx hospital. "D'Andre Walker, please."

A distracted middle-aged nurse typed and then shook her head. "No. Afraid not. He's in critical condition."

"Just one minute."

Steve moved toward the swinging entrance doors.

The nurse shifted to block his path. "Sir! I said no!"

Steve froze before her. "Please. I won't upset him. I promise. He'll want to see me."

She turned and peeked back through the rectangular windows into the ER. "...You go in one minute. And come right out."

"I will."

She walked back to her station, gazing off the other way.

Steve rushed into the ER.

D'Andre slept unattended in a little cubby, curtained off from the others. An oxygen mask strapped to his face, he looked peaceful. The medical machines beeped and purred.

Steve stepped up quietly, and he examined the boy. "D'Andre?"

D'Andre flopped his head over to the side, groggily opening his eyes. "Steve?"

"What happened?"

"Nothin'."

"Oh, man. I gotta find your doctor."

D'Andre grabbed Steve's wrist fast. "No. Just make me a promise."

"What?" Steve's eye began to water.

D'Andre stared up contemplatively. "Matter what happens, take down them assholes. And Dragomir too."

Steve crushed his eyelids shut, and he nodded.

"Then it's all good."

"It's all good."

"That's what I'm sayin'."

The reception nurse appeared at the entrance way. She feigned a cough in Steve's direction.

"Hang in there, man."

D'Andre released his grip. "What else can I do?"

Steve trudged back out of the ER.

TWENTY FIVE

Steve returned solemnly to his house. The place showed no signs of trouble, but he needed to check everywhere, now that they would be coming for him. He overturned his bed. Beneath it, sunk into the floorboards, was a steel safe. He dialed in the combination.

Inside the little safe he retrieved that wristwatch given to him by the President but never worn. He picked up a tiny syringe with black sparkling liquid inside of it. Once he examined the watch, he realized that he could fit the needle inside it if he just broke off most of the metal tip.

He clasped the silver watch to his wrist and set

the time. Reaching for the safe's door, its other contents arrested his attention. The photo album. He looked away quickly but it was too late. Despite his aversion, the photographs called again. He resumed his quest for meaning and place.

Cathy appeared so cute and alive and beautiful in those pictures, to go and die so young. He found playful shots before they had married. On a trip to the seashore they body-surfed together. The photos clicked all day along the boardwalk.

In between the waves, a sea creature brushed across Cathy's bare calf and she freaked out. Jellyfish, crab, fish, she didn't know. After a blood-curdling scream, she jumped into his arms for protection. Her body shivered and her eyes pressed closed. Her beautiful face squished up like a child's. When she didn't wear her glasses Cathy feared the strange even more. She hated it.

Steve searched below them in the silty green water, but he saw nothing.

"Hey." He smiled and squeezed her body gently. "It's okay. They're gone."

"They?"

"It. Whatever." With her clinging onto him in his arms, he carried her out of the sea and onto the sand.

Cathy set her feet down. "Oh my God, I told you I hate the ocean!" It was true. They never did return. Cathy always made excuses to avoid the beach, and Steve obliged her for the rest of her life.

TWENTY SIX

D r. Claude LaGrange stood at the podium and scanned the dozens of stern faces in the crowd seated at their banquet tables. He saw his colleagues as competitors. The ballroom was lit dimly, but a spotlight glared in his eyes.

LaGrange basked in this moment of opportunity, his chance to upend the status quo, which he had grown so tired of.

"I am formally announcing the detection of dark matter entanglement within cells of living organisms."

Jolts and restlessness fanned across the dining tables. Several reached for their wine glasses.

LaGrange sneered off at the far wall of the ballroom. "I have a novel experimental technique, which is unprecedented, and none of you, frankly, will be besting me to publication. My observations to date concern the conversion of dark matter to dark energy, and vice-versa. And so I say to you all, with absolute certainty, that the dawn of a new age of understanding the interplay of dark particles and living biological systems is currently before us."

After a chilly silence, an unseen elderly German chuckled in the darkness. Snickers radiated swiftly across the ballroom, until most of the physicists struggled to restrain themselves.

LaGrange whipped to his right, and he marched off the stage. Before slipping beyond the edge of the curtain he heard the gruff German octogenarian bellow, "Tell us when you pass peer review, Claude!"

LaGrange raised up his black-charred face from the concrete floor. In mounting confusion he pushed the steel desk off of his torso. The debris of his equipment had been tossed from the massive seismic event. Gasping rhythmically, to remain alive in the smoky atmosphere, his body tried to wriggle free, but the desk crushed his legs.

The basement crackled with sparks and flames from every direction. Electrical ribbons shot out from the power generator at the far wall. The flames seemed minor compared to the ideas shooting through his mind now. His body cried for more oxygen, but his will demanded results. It was all happening.

"The catalyst."

Where had it gone?

LaGrange extricated his leg, bleeding from the scrapes, and the pain nearly incapacitated him. He crawled forward through the wreckage pushing books and mangled metallic structures from his path.

As he approached the overturned particle accelerator, his organs felt baked like bread. His skin fried to crispiness. His mind, though, obsessed to locate his life's work somewhere splattered around that smoldering pile of debris.

On the filthy concrete, sparkling flickers rose from a black flowing liquid, one he had never before seen. His body wretched, collapsing from its own weight. His fingers lifted a sheet of metal to uncover more of the mysterious dark sparkling substance.

Events constantly popped around this black sludge, radioactive undoubtedly. Like a sparkler from a *Bastille Day* parade, the liquid crackled endlessly. Its surface appeared blacker than black, non-reflective, a hole in space-time. He thought to time the phenomenon and derive a half-life, but already he had lost track of time. His eyes would not focus properly as they teared up and closed on him. What anger at his useless anatomy.

LaGrange, with his face down on the floor inches above the black goo, stared amazed at his catalyst product. His stiff, burnt hand grabbed at a wayward glass beaker to store this new finding. With the edge of a piece of cardboard he gathered what he could find of the liquid. It ran down into the glass container. Each radioactive annihilation sparked within as well as outside of the glass barrier. Glass was permeable to it. He held it up to the streaming light of the basement window and he named it *Dark Matter Catalyst 1495-L.*

A tsunami of pain finally washed over LaGrange, and he could not persist. His body curled up on the cellar floor, shivering uncontrollably.

After the blackout, sometime later, LaGrange struggled to ascend the fractured staircase with his beaker in hand.

Steven Arkin still lay unconscious on a cot, strapped down conveniently. Oxygen and tubes kept him going for all this time.

LaGrange coughed and everything shook.

Desperate not to drop his prize discovery, he stabilized himself. His quaking hands retrieved an empty syringe from among the overturned medical paraphernalia. The needle sucked up the black catalyst. LaGrange's body jolted, bent over Arkin, slowly losing control of his own nervous system.

He gazed closely down at the syringe. His eyes watered, and he checked once again for those flashing pops, the signature of his catalyst, although his eyeballs started to spin. His catalyst acted as some gateway between the normal universe and its next iteration, a dark one indeed.

He injected Steven Arkin's arm.

TWENTY SEVEN

s the late news played live on a screen, Brett Holt announced to the viewing audience, "Tonight's guest, a chat with Supernatural Steven Arkin. Maybe he can shed a little light on the *Council* Interim President's upcoming address to the United Nations. You're not going to want to miss this exclusive interview. Tonight."

Steve clicked off the TV broadcast, and he inspected himself in his wall mirror. His body had taken some blows from that earlier fight in Africa. His burned chest healed somewhat, but it still felt damaged. His house in complete darkness, Steve strolled out of the sliding glass door into his yard. Checking his watch and the milky black night sky above, he jolted upward at a high speed.

The news studio broadcast tower sat in a sea of flickering skyscrapers in the center of midtown, Madison Avenue. Steve knew it well. Floating forward with caution, he remained suspicious that he was being watched. *How could they not be watching now?*

Far below in the city glare, streams of headlights flowed. Drivers crawled in ignorance of what was about to transpire. The moon nearly full, its face provided crisp reflected white light that painted the earth.

Snaking around slender towers of glass and steel, Steve located the network studio helipad and the rooftop entrance door.

From nowhere, bashed across the night and thrown into disarray, it was that one they called Stellar. He impacted and sent Steve tumbling end over end at such a high speed that all blurred.

With a grip on one ankle, Steve found himself spun and thrown clear out of the city's airspace. Darkened and dizzy, whipped again into an uncontrollable tailspin, Steve attempted to find his bearings. He searched for the moon as a reference in the spinning streaks of light.

Stellar pushed him rapidly over to the rural dark hills.

"Not smart, rodent."

Steve found an angle to head-butt Stellar in his arrogant face. The two separated, and he flew backwards.

Stellar rolled awkwardly past and half a mile above him.

Steve rushed up to take the fight to him.

The two brawled in the moonlight, bashing one another with little effect. Steve wailed at him with his fists full of primordial human anger.

Stellar blocked his blows, but he had slowed down a bit from his own disorientation.

A fist connected with Steve's face. Steve punched at the empty air.

Stellar was too fast to see.

Stellar grabbed hold at Steve's torso, and Steve elbowed down onto the back of his neck and then kicked him off.

Again Stellar rushed in at high speed, knocking Steve straight down toward the earth in a fierce vertical plummet.

Steve grabbed for Stellar's face. Fingers gouged

deep into his eyes.

"Aaaaaaa!"

Steve broke off with a knee, as Stellar blindly rocketed straight down into a mountain. When he impacted, it was a complete vaporization.

Searching below in the darkness Steve floated back to the earth. The crash had splattered his opponent across the sedimentary rock faces.

He rested on the mountainside to catch his bearings.

Stellar was gone, annihilated.

Steve overlooked the distant city glow, checking himself for injuries. His big transformation had kept its end of the bargain. Not a scratch on him.

TWENTY EIGHT

When the rocks above started to loosen their ancient hold, Dragomir presumed himself deceased. There was no kind of time measurement beneath the weight of the earth. He had long given up on ever being free again. No one would ever come for him intentionally. Centuries-long frustrations had rendered him as numb as the surrounding dirt. He had not even bothered to listen for decades, since the previous eruptions and earthquakes. There was nothing to sense. Existence was as empty a prospect as was the vastness of the universe.

When those tons of rock began to lift away,

Dragomir could actually hear the shovels chipping the stones above his resting place. His revelation was almost sufficient to prompt the semblance of an emotion.

Those churning, machine-powered excavators rumbled the ground. Their vibrations were nothing like he had ever experienced. Mechanized earth shakers pulled the rocks and the dirt from right off his back.

Those Chinese workmen had no idea what hit them.

Like a volcanic explosion, Dragomir burst again into the free air, unrestrained. The final ton of dirt shot up into the sky from off of his leather wings. Spreading out for the first time in three millennia, he surveyed the construction crew below him.

With meticulous vigilance, Dragomir murdered every last human workman involved and left no witnesses alive. Once free and soaring above the countryside, he made himself a new vow to hide in the darkest shadows of the night until circumstances tilted toward his favor. His most valuable lessons were internalized, and the half-dragon was ready to rule over everywhere and everything without the slightest mercy or restraint.

In Dragomir's presidential office, a full wall

consisted of television monitors from around the globe. Chinese, Russian, Indian, Pakistani, European, South American, and several were devoted to the United States' national news channels. Eastern US time clicked to 11:25pm, and Dragomir gazed impatiently at his glowing screens. Another tedious minute passed, and then two of the screens fell dark.

He grinned.

With precision he homed in on the breaking coverage, and with a flick of his finger he sent it up to the largest wall screen to bask in.

Breaking news interrupted. "Power failure takes down the eastern US electrical grid. Details emerging."

Dragomir touched a button, and he spoke. "M. Remember what we discussed?"

Pandora's vaporous tones echoed back and filled the cold stone corners of the fortress chamber. "We'll see," she said.

"Will we? What are you getting at?"

"Kid gloves, Dragomir," she said. "We're not dealing with dinosaurs."

"As you like."

Live news reports swiftly lit up screen after screen. Footage from a surveillance camera, a fence, a parking lot, and a man. The camera overlooked a massive transformer field, a major power generating plant. The man strolled right up to the camera and smiled.

The newsman said, "It appears to be the Supernatural Steven Arkin, and watch what he does next."

The man in the video lifted a pickup truck from the first parking row, and he threw it over the fence at the power station. When the vehicle crashed among the towering transformers they exploded in a series of white flashes of energy high into the night.

The news people reeled, an elder anchorman rambling in confusion. "Oh my. This is highly disturbing footage. And now a full third of the United States remains in darkness, a cascading power failure that has knocked out several of our affiliate stations. This is terrible. We are going to need answers immediately."

As the security camera rolled, the man in the video tossed another car into the burning chaos, and the electrical discharge blinded the sensor, which soon blacked out.

The woman in the co-anchor chair said,

"Terrifying."

The anchorman bellowed, "Is America now vulnerable to terrorism by Supernaturals?"

Dragomir touched another button on his desk. "Yes. I'll need to respond now. Put this through. Thank you."

Live news showed a satellite image of a darkened east coast. Hysterical staff bustled around in their news studio.

A new video stream arrived from the floor of Congress. An angry, old white Congressman frothed at the center podium. "My constituents are literally in the dark! While incontrovertible evidence points at deliberate, malicious sabotage by one of those Supernaturals. One Arkin, Steven Arkin. He's committed a blatant Treasonous act against these here United States. And we need to know right now what is the President doin' about it?"

A rival congressman shouted, "Will the gentleman yield?"

"No sir! Not until this President declares a national emergency!"

Dragomir faded up the lights in his office and he re-positioned himself before his own camera. "Yes, can you see me now?"

"Yes sir," came back a disembodied voice from the other side of the world.

A security camera image, of Steve Arkin smiling, froze on Dragomir's gigantic wall monitor.

In the TV studio, a portly, bearded academic had been labeled tonight's *EXPERT ON SUPERNATURALS.*

The news moderator jumped into action.

"Welcome to this fast breaking story. A rogue Supernatural, what do we know so far? Professor?"

The seated little man held up a copy of his book for some reason. Behind him, Dragomir sat patiently on the screen, looming over them and awaiting his turn to speak.

The self-proclaimed expert talked with his hands, for emphasis. "What created this *Lab Rat?* This has never been made clear to the public. There are theories, but I don't think that's going to cut it given these recent, unforgivable actions."

Dragomir parted his clawed hands gently. "If I may?"

The studio paused for him. The others went silent, and they all turned respectfully back to face the big screen.

Dragomir spoke softly, "It appears that Steven Arkin's mental capacity has deteriorated due to the transformative process he underwent."

The expert pointed at his book. "In my book I ask these very same fundamental questions. What happens if Supernaturals misuse their power? Or snap? Or not even intentionally as we've clearly seen today, but just accidentally. Are they too powerful? That's the question we face as a species."

Dragomir sat stoically. "Please don't judge all Supernaturals based upon Steven Arkin's reprehensible actions. After all, he was just a common human who subsequently was altered to become something that he is not."

The anchorman interrupted. "Gentlemen? In your opinions, just how much danger are we in right now from the Steven Arkin threat?"

Scrolling text below them on the screen repeatedly asked the same question.

TWENTY NINE

Steve felt internally disoriented from the impacts and the beating Stellar had inflicted on him. He shook himself off, and he rose up on that dim mountainside in the moonlight. This was the final resting place of his opponent. Up and back toward the city lights, his interview was still scheduled in just minutes time. He needed to hurry back to the news studio to keep true to his word. That was one thing Steve valued above all others, keeping his word.

When the power failed across the horizon, he jolted back and struggled to understand. The entire city and beyond descended into darkness, save for the headlights and a few emergency generators providing soft red glows in isolated pockets. A power failure of this magnitude could lead to chaos and rioting across the metropolitan area. It was something to behold at five-thousand feet, but it felt truly ominous as to what might come next.

Steve floated toward the black buildings, listening to the symphony of honking horns below. The news tower went dark. Television was off the air.

He decided instead to target Pandora's dark silver skyscraper, where a few emergency red flashers signaled to planes from her rooftop.

His fingertip tapped softly on her glass penthouse egress.

Pandora strolled into the loft below, lighting up the foliage with her personal aura. She floated up to the other side of the glass, to face him. Her softly pulsing blue energy reflected off the window pane.

Steve gazed in plaintively. "Can we talk a little while? No sex."

Pandora smirked, and she pushed open her massive window for him.

Steve flew inside. The two arrived on the floor together. Candles illuminated her loft garden. Her big cats crept silently in the shadows of the flickering jungle foliage.

Pandora's eyes gazed at his face. "So, what happened to you?"

"They're trying to kill me."

"Oh? Who?"

Steve collapsed onto her plush couch, lazing back to escape reality. These fights had indeed taken a toll. He felt disturbed, his energy flows curtailed. He had weakened in that dark realm, which no one understood. His entangling had strained and deformed from the violence.

Pandora's face brightened with golden light. "Can I ask you something, Steve?"

THIRTY

It was within the Presidential office of Woden, before the rise of Dragomir. Pandora sat across his desk.

Gungnir stowed in its designated place, Woden fixed his good eye on Miss Melt's radiating face and breathed her mesmerizing energy in.

She could see herself shimmering in the reflection of Woden's eyeball. Pandora decided then that she would brighten, and the entire room seared with her emitted light. Woden's wolves snapped to attention. His crows gazed quizzically over at the two of them.

"So Woden? Do you love me?"

Like a nuclear detonation, Woden ceased being present. The *Council* President became a statue, his mouth locked in a pleasant smile. His mind had traveled so far and so fast as to be severed from his present reality.

Pandora softened back to normal and rose herself up silently.

"Mister President? How about if I just get the door?"

Woden's white wolves yawned, lazing about on mats. His crows glanced curiously over, as Woden beamed with delight.

Pandora smiled. "You do love me."

Gracefully she glided to the stone chamber door. When she released the mechanism, Dragomir stood in the doorway alone. She nodded softly.

He crept inside the chamber with her.

"Woden?" she announced playfully. "Dragomir has something he wants to tell you."

Dragomir stepped forward, as Pandora kept watch on the pets. Woden's wolves remained docile, but now their interest had been piqued.

Woden remained smiling and gawking at the pictures in his mind.

Dragomir slid cautiously toward the large desk, his nervousness evident.

Pandora coughed and amped her colors to cold silver. "Oh look at me, Woden. I'm all tingly."

The first white wolf rose on its paws with a curious apprehension.

Dragomir stepped again toward Gungnir. "Can he hear?"

"He hears what I want him to hear."

Dragomir's reptilian eyes widened, and he turned longingly toward the silver spear.

Pandora lazed back on a couch near the door, casually raising her feet.

She watched as Dragomir lunged at Gungnir. Woden's two Ravens took flight to protect it.

Dragomir grabbed for the spear, and with it sliced the first raven in half. It evaporated in a puff of blue lightning.

The second Raven shot in toward the dragon man, and he grabbed the bird by its throat. His claw crushed down and squeezed all the energy from it.

Pandora backed up to the far wall, watching quietly as the white wolves sprang at them. Both pounced with a thunderous momentum. They split up.

The first came roaring right at her with its teeth bared.

Pandora instantly slammed the wolf up against he wall by its throat. With her dagger, she impaled it. The beast squirmed maniacally as she twisted in the blade.

Dragomir launched Woden's spear at the second beast. It pierced straight through long-ways, and the animal disintegrated in a hail of blue beams.

The two co-conspirators whipped back to face Woden in his Presidential chair. Still he sat smiling away at the blank wall.

Pandora composed herself, while. Dragomir rushed over to retrieve Gungnir.

The dragon even seemed to have achieved a level of excitement. "He's not moved a muscle!"

Pandora relaxed, and she slid down again onto the couch.

"He loves me."

Across the room, Dragomir towered. He gauged the weight of the spear in his claws. "It never misses?"

"Never."

She watched Dragomir admire the weapon from top to bottom like a child at Christmas, teasing little blue sparks from the weapon with the tip of his claw.

Without urgency, he strolled behind Woden's chair and lowered himself into an appropriate stance, grasping the spear to throw.

"Not my father." Dragomir let the weapon go, and it harpooned Woden through his chair, through his unprotected back, and lodged in his rib cage.

The blast of blue energy was massive.

Pandora guarded her face. Shock waves radiated out from Woden's body in all directions. Things in the office were blown asunder.

Woden, the presumed god and self-proclaimed leader of earth's Supernaturals, turned to stone.

When the damage had finalized, she watched Dragomir march over and yank the spear back out. Woden's earthly remains crumbled to ash and dust. It seemed a bit distasteful. And the office needed a good cleaning.

Dragomir ripped a decorative drape from the wall to wipe the residue from his new friend Gungnir.

"There's been a change of leadership," he hissed as he nodded at her, and she nodded back.

THIRTY ONE

Steve's options were fading away.

He'd just killed Stellar. Although in self-defense, he didn't feel all that innocent about gouging a man's eyes out, even one as malevolent as Stellar. Maybe he wasn't a man. If Supers were something else, then there was no way of knowing what laws guided them, if any. He was trapped now in his own black hole of unknowing.

They were coming. That much was clear.

He reached out to the only entity whom he might have a shot with. She was too pristine, too pure to fall in with the likes of the Barbarian and Nukeman. They had a relationship, as odd and strained as it was.

Steve's mind reeled as he admitted to her that he was running scared and confused.

Pandora welcomed him into her home. She sat him down and even mixed him a drink, which she seemed obsessed with. Her body glowed in a pure white shimmer like an angel. Although Miss Melt always glowed, she seemed like the only beacon of purity left in this mangled wasteland of egomaniacs and the lies that inevitably came out of their mouths.

"Steve," she said, and the room flared even brighter.

White light everywhere pinned open his eyes.

She said, "Do you love me?"

Steve gazed into that immaculate luminescent face, an unimaginable goddess, someone who shouldn't exist.

Pandora bathed the entire jungle-themed suite in her pulsing white flare.

Steve jolted, unsure of his thoughts, as the room washed out in waves of energy.

"Do you love me, Steve?"

Her haunting voice lingered and echoed through his brain. The world exploded like a firework finale.

Far away, transported on the waves of memory, he saw Cathy on their wedding day. She was still Cathy Ferguson, about to become Arkin.

He thought he could hear Pandora. "Just like Woden. You men are so goddamned easy."

Kissing Cathy. Twirling her around in her long white gown. A sparkling ring, a reception of friends, dancing without a care, toasts of bubbly, jokes from everyone. The party raged long into the night.

In bed at that hotel, Cathy said, "We're married now," as she jumped to straddle him. Like a social taboo had been lifted from her, some mental cage unlocked, she grabbed at his body uninhibited.

In the hospital, Cathy lay devastated, reduced to a sweaty mess. Michael was born. Steve lifted the newborn gently, a little squirming monkey. He absorbed the tiny, contorted face with so much potential. So much responsibility overwhelmed him.

Steve sat adjacent Cathy at her eye doctor appointment. Again and again, prescription after prescription. Her glasses went thicker and more cumbersome.

The rain, the windshield, Cathy fought the

steering wheel to the end. Their car slid forward, and then sideways, and then into the nothingness. Through space, they were over the edge in free fall. And then her scream.

A tear rolled down Steve's cheek, and then another and another. He realized again where he was.

So strange.

Pandora, an immortal, casually mixed herself another cocktail over at her bar. Her illuminated hair flowed with soft green flickers. Her delicate lips sipped at the concoction unaware that he had turned his head again to study her.

"I don't love you, Pandora."

Taken aback, she dropped her glass and its contents to the floor.

"Like hell you don't."

In a flash of temper she flared blindingly.

Steve rose from her couch, shielding his eyes with his palm. "The only woman I ever loved was Cathy Ferguson."

Pandora's body shot shock waves of green pulses at him, which he tried to ignore.

He refused to acknowledge her tantrum. "It's my fault they died." He shook his head and wiped his cheek.

"She couldn't see. I. I was drunk. Selfish. I killed them. I killed them all."

The nerve endings reconnected, his spine felt human again, too human, and too vulnerable.

Miss Melt retreated back in her confusion toward the hallway. Her agitated cats snarled, and crept over to protect her.

Steve stumbled to the side, lost in his recovered memories. Then he looked up for the escape route.

"You killed Woden?"

Pandora calmed to a pleasant peach spectrum, moving toward him again. "It's not too late to join us. Make amends. Dragomir likes you, in spite of yourself."

Steve shook his head with disgust, and he flew up and out of Pandora's window portal back into the wild.

THIRTY TWO

Steve Arkin flew across the dark, dirty river toward the Bronx Children's Hospital. By morning, the east coast of America remained without its electricity grid. The sun peeked from the ocean, as the headlights of the cars below shone up from dark crevices. Crashes and scrapes at numerous intersections, drivers battled to push ahead of one another in the chaos.

As Steve floated in toward the brick block of a building, he saw bright yellow police tape stretched across broken glass. Below the hospital, parked on the street, a pair of blue police cars sat quietly.

Steve landed immediately on the sidewalk, and

he walked up to the nearest police car.

The two officers panicked. Doors flew open, and they jumped out of their car grabbing for guns.

Steve halted in place. "What's going on here?"

"Freeze!"

His partner called into a radio. "It's Arkin!"

Steve looked to the building entrance.

More police rushed out of the front doors with their guns drawn, all of them dashing straight at him.

Without warning, they blasted from four different guns, knocking Steve backward.

"Stop!" he yelled.

Bullets bashed his skin and battered him violently.

"Wait a minute!"

He jumped up into the air and past the rooftop.

The cops continued firing in his direction, until he escaped over the corner of the hospital's roof. Above the fray, Steve spun in befuddlement. He checked his skin for gunshot wounds. They pinged unpleasantly and had left little red bruises. The holes in his new shirt annoyed him too.

Soaring back toward the skyscrapers of Manhattan, he kept an eye below for signs of pursuit.

His mind careened. That sixth-floor window was broken in. *D'Andre Walker might now be tangled up in this mess.*

Across the radio spectrum, Steve heard loud transmissions. Snippets of conversations echoed around his eardrums.

"Copy. Dogcather 2 is radar contact tally-ho."

"He's bulls-eye one-one-six, seventy-six now, three thousand."

"I'm a mile and a half in trail, closing."

Steve twisted about to find a pair of F-18s diving at him. Their radar-guided missiles fired.

The weapons turned as he did. One of the rockets hit and blasted him across the sky in a massive orange fire burst.

The two F-18s rocketed past him.

From the fire and into free fall Steve tumbled out of control toward the buildings. He held his head as he dropped down at the Bronx street. Returning to consciousness, and charred black from the explosion, he saw the ground rising fast.

Laterally, Steve dashed between tall tenement buildings.

The two fighter planes came about again behind him. Both of them fired another round of air-to-air missiles.

Steve dodged with a sharp turn down a side street. The missiles exploded on the avenue, tossing parked cars about. It was a war zone.

He shot vertically past the attacking planes, behind them, and off into the stratosphere. Into the clouds as fast as he could. He poured on the speed until he was rid of the Air Force, at least temporarily.

Turning north, he plummeted into a valley between mountain peaks. Over the treetops, and through a green farm region, he homed in on a tiny, remote pond. There he splashed down near the shore, and he washed off his burns and the tatters of his shirt in the pond water. Skin had singed and looked discolored. It didn't hurt, but he felt awkward damaging his body so severely.

Out from the pond, he trudged toward a familiar log cabin. Inside his cabin, he ripped off the remnants of his clothes. Exhausted and throbbing, Steve collapsed onto a shabby plaid couch. His remote controller clicked on a television set. Chaos poured into the room from across the broadcast spectrum.

Cars still burned in New York City from the government's own F-18 attack, also blamed on him. A young reporter woman standing before the fire said, "A scene of awesome destruction, in the authorities' latest attempt to put a halt to Supernatural Steven Arkin's reign of terror."

He shrugged in disbelief.

Even their graphics people were on point with *The Hunt for a Rogue Supernatural*.

Steve flicked the channel.

Back at the Bronx Children's Hospital D'Andre Walker's grandfather arrived and was interviewed. "Please bring D'Andre back, Mister Arkin. He's so sick, he can't handle any more." Tears halted the old man. His graphic read, *Gerald Walker, Grandfather of D'Andre Walker.*

Steve flicked the channel again.

A less-than-credible reporter approached an upscale house, identified as the *Home of Erica Tate*. The front door opened. Little Erica Tate, with her white bald head, stood with her parents behind her.

The man with the microphone pushed it in at the girl. "Do you believe on your flight with Lab Rat Arkin that he ever touched you inappropriately?"

Erica's face twisted with confusion. "Whaaaaaaaaaaat???"

Video cut back to another news studio.

A pundit newsreader took over and said, "Obviously in shock, an innocent, sick child tries to make sense of it all."

Steve clicked again to the next horror show, until he couldn't stomach any more. With frustration he stood up.

Images showed an electrical power station, its hub destroyed. Workmen attempted to make snap repairs. A media circus surrounded the electrical site. Graphics announced *Supernatural Sabotage Now a National Security Threat.* The channel replayed the previous night's security camera footage. Stepping up to the booth and smiling, it looked like Steve destroyed the electrical plant, and for no discernible reason whatsoever.

He jumped forward at his TV, his nose right up to the screen, taking a good look at himself.

Another professional talker chattered. "The nation awaits Interim *Council of Power* President Dragomir's much-anticipated speech today, at twelve o'clock noon at the United Nations building in midtown Manhattan."

Steve stormed back to his cabin's bathroom to

take a shower and compose himself. The larger world
made no sense whatsoever.

THIRTY THREE

Pandora stormed down her hallway and out into her penthouse loft. Looking up, her aura seared in red.

"What the hell now?"

Sharp shadows raked across the row of glass above. At the windows, the figures gathered in a bunch. Dragomir, Barby the Barbarian, while Nukeman carried the little sick human, D'Andre Walker, in his arms.

Pandora opened the portal, and they all pushed inside like an invading guerrilla army.

"Why the hell would you bring *him* here?"

Dragomir flapped his leathery wings into a compact fold behind him. "And a beautiful morning to you too, Miss Melt."

Barby stomped out into her hallway and inspected the suite.

Pandora snapped at him. "Hey. Watch your step, ox. What if someone saw him?"

Dragomir quipped, "That sort of thing should no longer concern us. Arkin remains a loose end though."

D'Andre looked up and smiled at Dragomir, annoying him.

Nukeman pushed the boy over at Pandora's legs. "You take him."

"Uggh." She shook her head.

"That insect," said Dragomir, "could be of use to us if you can work your magic on its little mind."

She gasped. "Oh, are you serious?"

Dragomir scoffed. "If it's still working, that is. Your spells."

"Watch it." Pandora growled indignantly, her hair flaming to crimson.

Dragomir smiled like a mechanical puppet. "Well, you did have Arkin all to yourself last evening, no?"

With swirls of orange flame, she glowed furiously. "Put him in there."

Nukeman yanked D'Andre to a door and shoved him inside the den.

Dragomir's creepy crocodile eyes stared back coldy. "Why can't we watch? Afraid you've lost your touch?"

"I'm protecting you from overspill," she whispered through clenched teeth. "Once I turn it up, I won't be responsible for how you're affected."

She whipped her shoulders about and sauntered into the den like an enflamed ballerina, illuminating the walls as she passed them.

Dragomir followed her inside. "Wait here," he told the others.

Pandora sized up D'Andre on the floor.

"Quickly," Dragomir bickered. "I've still got my speech to write." He latched the door behind him.

D'Andre sat huddled on the floor in the corner, his back leaned up against the white walls.

Pandora nodded at Dragomir. "You'd better not look directly."

"Princess," he replied, "your love potion is of no concern to me, whatsoever."

The two Supernaturals towered over the boy as he slumped down pathetically. His eyes crawled slowly up, and he looked like he might just die right there and then.

Pandora cracked her knuckles. The room flashed to a blinding white, and she rose into the air a few inches for added oomph. "D'Andre? Hello? Listen to me."

All her internal forces poured out in the white light, attacking the boy in spiraling threads of luminescence. It felt so good again to wield her primal energies at the universe.

The kid squinted to block her light, but the room filled entirely like a swimming pool.

Pandora smiled knowingly down on him. "Do you love me?"

Tethers of white shot from her hair right through D'Andre's skull. The rush jolted his body, and he collapsed all the way to the floor.

"That's enough," she said. Her bare feet touched back down to the floorboards, and she relaxed. The den returned to normalcy.

Dragomir watched curiously, behind her. "Well?"

Pandora knelt to softly stroke the kid's head.

D'Andre opened his eyes again. "I'm sorry, Miss Pandora. The only lady I love is my mama."

"Your mother?!" She bellowed. In a rage, she

jumped up, her colors flaring chaotically.

"Mmm." D'Andre righted himself and sat up. "She died. In that plane crash."

Pandora held her head, and her teeth ground. She floundered past Dragomir toward the door. As she passed the reptile, she imagined what might happen if she just reached out and snatched that spear from off his back and harpooned him with it.

Dragomir cocked his reptilian head, and he glared down on the little human with a grin.

"Plane crash? Really?"

THIRTY FOUR

D'Andre Walker was powerless. Barely conscious, he wasn't sure how much longer he could care about this world at all. It was over for him anyway. The darkness was catching up fast. It just annoyed him how hard it was to keep breathing. It would be better if he had his oxygen mask. But they didn't care.

Dragomir snatched him up whole in his cold freaky reptile claws. Before he knew it, they flew out of the building again over the city. He was high in the sky, but he just wanted to sleep.

Across the blue day, D'Andre wrestled to remain secure, as the lizard king dove quickly back toward the ground.

D'Andre's head flopped around in the breeze. He arrived at the nearest airport. Parked little Cessna planes sat silently in their own parking lot.

Dragomir wrenched open a cockpit door on the first one.

D'Andre was dumped into the pilot's seat. He slumped over away from the agitated dragon man, and he looked to all the controls.

Pandora landed in front of the plane. He saw her through the windshield.

When the door slammed shut, D'Andre jolted.

Dragomir ripped all the cables tying the plane down to the earth.

Trapped inside the Cessna cockpit, D'Andre felt the plane wrench violently into the air. Tilted forward and back, he reached for his seat belt. Weakly, he struggled to latch the metal pieces together. They clicked, and he gasped for breath. Outside the glass, the ground disappeared. The little plane shot up thousands of feet above the city until it slowed down and hovered there.

D'Andre pressed back into the pilot's chair as hard as he could, and he stared helplessly out across the landscape over the Metropolis. His stomach felt on the verge of giving out or throwing up or something.

Dragomir's claw held the supporting brace just outside the cockpit window. With his other hand he ripped open the plastic window from the cockpit door.

"All you need do is to tell Steven Arkin that what you really want is him to make peace with us." Dragomir shook the plane around for emphasis. "Are you listening to me?"

D'Andre held the steering wheel tightly, but his body battered back and forth from the shock waves. He wasn't sure he could speak.

The Cessna teetered and swayed in the air.

Dragomir's snout pressed up to the side window. "Or else join your parents, boy. What's it to be?" His reptilian pupils peered in through the window hole.

D'Andre panted, and he tried to regain control of himself. He latched onto the steering wheel to steady his body in the shifting aircraft that felt like *Jello*.

Dragomir wrenched the plane again.

"Answer me!"

D'Andre, dizzy from the motion, looked across the plane's controls and dials. He turned to face Dragomir.

His own teeth grit, and he glared back into Dragomir's eyes.

"Kiss my ass."

Dragomir flinched with a disgusted grumble. His claw tossed the plane away into the abyss.

D'Andre screamed.

The Cessna dropped back toward the ground.

He yanked at the steering wheel, jammed his foot down onto the pedal. The plane spun around, spiraled out of control, dropping faster toward the ground.

"Aaaaaaaaaaaaaaa!"

Nothing D'Andre did made the slightest difference. The dead aircraft flopped out of control in a corkscrew plummet toward the approaching buildings.

He closed his eyes, and he calmed himself.

Taking refuge in the darkness, D'Andre remembered his mom and his pop. He remembered what it was like before he got sick. He remembered his grandpops, and how they went out to the movies. They shopped for his new sneakers. He remembered Christmas time when they were all together eating baked turkey with stuffing and how they let him try wine for the first time. He remembered being in school, how life used to be regular, and he had a couple of friends that would joke with him, and it wasn't so bad at all. Now he forgot all their names. It had been so long. He liked it when life was regular. He liked the idea of just being like everybody else, watching TV, playing baseball and basketball, going to school, playing with his friends.

In total silence, D'Andre opened his eyes.

He was hanging upside down restrained by his seat belt, dangling in mid air.

Dragomir stood there on the street, holding the plane up. His ugly dinosaur face beamed back through the front windshield of the Cessna.

"I thought I'd ask once more, just to be certain."

Dragomir blasted the plane right back up to a high altitude, and he flipped it over to be up again.

D'Andre flopped over helplessly in his seat. He was too weak and sick to keep his head from rolling around aimlessly. The assault had worn him out and drained his remaining energy reserves. He would have threw up, but there was nothing in his stomach.

He knew this was the end.

Dragomir paused in the open air for another speech.

"We'll try this *one final time*."

Pandora, glowing like the yellow sun, flew over to him. She stopped in front of the Cessna's windshield.

"Really, Dragomir?"

The dragon scoffed back at her. "Are you going soft on me now, Melty?"

D'Andre's mouth drooled, and he wiped the spit away onto the seat.

The plane teetered in Dragomir's right claw, dancing to and fro.

Pandora said to him, "This is beneath even you."

Dragomir stared back at her like a gangsta.

D'Andre could only watch, slumped half over.

Dragomir huffed. "Do not forget the central role you've played in our new natural order."

D'Andre grabbed onto the steering wheel again. His insides were so agitated, but there was nothing in there. They hadn't fed him at all.

Miss Pandora tilted her head. "Leave the boy alone already."

D'Andre heaved onto his shirt, and his body spasmed.

Dragomir toyed with the plane a bit more, waving it about nonchalantly.

D'Andre jerked left and right, as they argued

outside the cockpit.

"There are eight billion!" yelled Dragomir. "None of us has yet attempted to endure a thermonuclear event. I don't relish the thought of being the first. Do you?"

She rolled her glowing white eyes, and she assumed a soft pink tone. "Exaggerate much?"

"Fourteen thousand nine hundred and seventeen atomic devices under the human's control."

"And?" She just kept staring back at Dragomir.

He jolted. "And Woden let the primate plague spiral completely out of control. Peace with them? Insanity."

She said, "We've done well enough so far."

"We kept their herds culled throughout the millennia, and now we're to try unconditional peace? Look what they do with it. They breed like roaches. No. Woden and his sentimentality had to go."

Pandora flew in beside him. "Draggy. Don't you have better things to do? Important things more worthy of your attentions?"

D'Andre studied them, as Dragomir seemed to calm again. The Cessna still teetered in his claw.

"Yes. I must prepare my words." He tossed the

plane away.

D'Andre screamed, "Ahhhhh!!!!"

His hands attempted to fight the controls. The plane leveled out, but then seemed to jet off in its own direction. As he slumped down in his seat, the Cessna slowed to a stop.

Through the side window he saw her. Pandora held the wing in one hand. She ripped off the door and tossed it away down below. When she pulled D'Andre out into her arms, he watched the plane drop toward the city streets.

She flew off, and he held onto her. Her skin buzzed like electricity.

Pandora sighed. "Wouldn't it have been nicer to just tell him what he wanted to hear?"

"I guess."

She soared back over the urban landscape toward her skyscraper.

D'Andre clung onto her glowing shoulder, half amazed and half ready to give up on life altogether. He knew his time was short. Any more shocks like that, and he would just go to sleep forever.

Drifting off in a stupor, he heard Pandora's blender whiz loudly in the kitchen.

She dropped in fruit and revved it up. Occasionally, she peeked around a dark green leaf to check up on him. As she chopped up stuff, she joked to herself.

D'Andre slid down on her couch. The blackness came again.

Miss Melt revved the machine a couple more times and called, "How can you sleep through this? I'm doing this for you."

D'Andre jerked to consciousness. "Huh?"

She hovered over him. "Just. Try this. This is the good stuff. Drink it." She jammed a smoothie into his face.

"Okay." D'Andre took the glass and sipped.

"More. More. There's plenty." Pandora glowed in aqua and violet, which swirled like she evolved from moment to moment. Maybe she cared.

D'Andre guzzled her concoction down.

Miss Melt shouted over her shoulder, "Lynx! Ocelot! What have I told you?"

Red radiated from her face. The prowling cats took notice. A bobcat sprinted through the loft and swiped at the other two. They were off to the races. Surface to surface, the cats jumped over the couches.

D'Andre ducked to keep a low profile.

"Dammit, I said stop it!" Pandora's voice coiled around the loft. The three cats froze in mid-battle. She rushed over to poke the ocelot on the top of his forehead.

He immediately lay down, eyes locked open and mesmerized.

"Who's next?"

The bobcat sat obediently.

D'Andre stirred. "Why don't you give 'em, like, real names?"

"I. Did."

Heaving up the smoothie, D'Andre vomited all over himself and over her sparkling white marble floor.

"Ohhhhh." Pandora exhaled with exaggeration. "Why me?"

"I'm sorry, Miss Pandora," he gurgled. "Sorry."

"You are the life of the party."

"I. I'll clean it up." D'Andre jerked to stand.

"Yeah. Do."

Her golden index finger pointed off past a row of red flowers toward the kitchen. D'Andre shuffled out to look for a way to wipe it up.

THIRTY FIVE

Inside his lakeside cabin, Steve Arkin had showered and scrubbed himself clean. He tossed away the burnt, shredded clothing into the trash. Still sliding on a pair of new socks, he kept one eye trained across the room for news updates.

"BREAKING."

His TV showed a nuclear power plant perched on the rocky Pacific coast of Southern California. The daytime anchor woman rushed through her announcement, "Breaking news. Supernatural Steven Arkin has been sighted at the nuclear power generating station at San Luis Obispo, California, where he is now engaged in a fierce stand-off with the station's security detail."

Steve rocketed up and through the roof of his cabin splintering the old wood and sending pieces flying off into the forest. He soared at maximum speed toward space in a southwestern beeline across the continental United States.

San Diego to the left, Los Angeles right, and somewhere in the middle, he had to set down.

It was not impossible to feel sensations from the disturbances below, multiple Supernaturals. Swirling dark clouds stirred up fields. The energy disturbances called him like sonar.

Steve descended fast and spotted the nuclear generating station. Then he could hear all the gunshots. Rapid-fire rang out.

Already, one of the cooling towers had knocked sideways at an angle. National Guard trucks arrived, and soldiers poured out around the outer chain-link fence.

Bullets ricocheted off the chrome. Sparks flashed.

Steve flew straight in toward the entanglement of silver pipes and metal structures. There he saw his alter ego wrench a giant water tank from its supports and lift it overhead to launch in the direction of the security guards.

"Hey Shifty!" Steve yelled.

Rocketing in behind the other, his fist sent the impostor flying across the compound. The water tank crashed and spilled contaminated water everywhere.

Steve set down to inspect the damage to the equipment. Steam hissed from severed pipes. Sirens squealed. He had no idea how much time remained to prevent a meltdown.

Shifty returned to his regular self, as he climbed back up to his knees.

Security guards scrambled for cover, still shooting wildly at the two Supers. The military surrounded them.

As Shifty rose back into the air, Steve tackled him. The two wrestled through the metal labyrinth of industrial plumbing, damaging pipes and catwalks as they brawled. Shifty punched fast and hard. Steve wrestled him around, and tried to secure him in a headlock.

Suddenly, Barby and Nukeman descended into the plant to join in the fight.

Nukeman's eyes blazed.

The wall adjacent Steve flared into a melted

metallic goo. Paint caught fire. Steve dove for cover around a corner.

"Raaaa!" The Barbarian roared, and he ripped a massive pipe to wield as a bat. "Come on, Rat Boy!"

Barby swung his pipe and flattened a guard shack.

Nukeman melted a liquid storage tank above where Steve had ducked in to hide. Spent fuel rods and radioactive waste water gushed out all over him and around the concrete yard.

Shifty flew overhead to trap Steve below him, while the Barbarian rushed in for a final bashing.

Steve looked to the Pacific, and he fled out to the water. The three Supers pursued him into the blue, as the nuke plant gushed steam and contamination from the extensive damage they had caused.

Sometime later, Steve slid quietly ashore at a wharf and up onto an old abandoned dock. His clothes were slimed with oily water. He had made it halfway to L.A., and it seemed an inconspicuous enough spot. The rotting pier seemed deserted.

A twentieth-century payphone sat on the desolate roadside lot.

"Who's this?" she said.

Pandora's voice was drowned out by a food blender.

Steve huffed disgustedly. "You know who it is."

"I need to change my number."

"Where's D'Andre Walker?"

"I've got him," she said.

He nodded. "Can you just drop him off at a hospital? Any hospital?"

"Sorry, Steve." With a click, she hung up.

THIRTY SIX

Miss Melt descended from a clear blue sky in the bright sun. A horse-drawn carriage rambled below on a rutty dirt path. The vehicle was adorned with royal insignias and flags.

At seeing her above him, the driver trembled. He whipped his animals as hard as he could in a feeble attempt to escape her.

She simply floated down before them, gazed into their eyes, and they trotted to a halt. The frantic human continued to whip and crossed himself in his terrified delirium.

Pandora's shimmering bare feet touched down

onto the rumps of the nearest horse pair, and she flashed her eyes to silence the crazed little man. "Who is your king?"

The driver's hands shook uncontrollably, as they clung to a rosary necklace.

"Answer."

"My lord is King Philip."

"Is he old, young? Attractive?"

"He is twenty-two years, my lady." The terrorized driver stared down to the right, and then squeezed shut his eyes to avoid seeing her.

"Has he a wife? Are you without a queen?"

"My lord is engaged to be wed."

"Oh. Unfortunate, for the girl. Very well. Remember nothing."

Her energy blinded him in a long flare, and she soared over his head and toward a small cluster of puffy clouds in the distance.

Miss Melt eventually arrived above the castle of King Philip. There she hovered like a second sun, observing the little creatures. Her pores gushed raw white energy for the sake of spectacle, which humans were so fond of.

The dumbfounded serfs gathered below in the

courtyard. Many dropped to their knees. Others slunk back into the recesses to hide themselves and their children.

Pandora's white feet set down on the cobblestone road before a line of crossbow-armed royal guards. Her skin faded back to normalcy.

"Greetings," she said.

They whispered in terrified snippets. "Is she an angel?"

"What shall we do?"

As Pandora strolled ahead in her flowing silver gown, the men retreated and cleared a swath for her. Jittery hands hovered at the handles of their swords.

"Is she a demon?"

"A witch?"

Pandora announced, "I bring thee only good tidings."

As she spun slowly, she smiled on the simple creatures.

They stared at her illumination and became more pliant. Focusing her attention on one old soldier with the most elaborate colors, she curtsied before him and gazed deeply into his face.

"I bring important news for King Philip, and it is

for his ears only."

The disturbed commander nodded awkwardly, and he set off to retrieve his King. Minutes later, the young Philip appeared. He was moderately attractive and wore a beard. Peeking from behind his shifting wall of bodyguards, he cowered.

Their entire society had screeched to a halt. All the peasants gawked from every available position around the castle courtyard.

The king stepped to within fifty feet of Pandora, and he called, "I am Philip, the sovereign of these lands. Who are you?"

Pandora curtsied to him. "My lord, I seek an audience to discuss great projects that will make your kingdom the envy of all of Europe." As she caught his glance, her flaring eyes burrowed into his mind, and her energy snared him from across the yard.

King Philip's face glowed pleasantly, and he pushed out in front of his guards. "That sounds quite marvelous."

"Indeed it will be, sire. Shall we retreat to more private accommodations? And I will share my wondrous gifts with thee?"

The bishop, a short sweaty man off to the side of

the King's guards, shook his head confusedly and he called out, "Are you an angel from God? Or are you from the Devil?"

Gasps.

Heads shook, and people retreated a step. The crowd froze in silence.

Pandora smirked, as she located him in the audience. "And if there were neither?"

The bishop repeated the words. "If there were neither?" He hid himself behind the soldiers. "Is this blasphemy?"

She smiled. "It is a question for your question."

The King stepped out commandingly. "Hold! I shall speak with this good lady and all questions shall be answered in time." Philip trotted forward and presented himself before her.

"I am honored, your majesty."

"Come. We shall discuss your plans, together."

"I am indeed charmed." Pandora bowed her head and strutted forward with King Philip into his castle. They ascended several winding staircases.

Within the royal bed chamber, Pandora took up a position facing him.

King Philip breathed in deeply, mesmerized by

her presence.

Pandora's eyes meandered around the room and took in the royal flourishes. "I have decided that I am a queen."

"Oh?"

"Yes, it is the only solution for us."

"For us?"

"Your queen." Her fingers untied her silken gown, and it slid off her and to her feet, leaving her naked and pulsing with soft peach energy.

Philip's eyes fixed involuntarily on her glowing body.

Pandora stepped right out of her garment toward him. "You like me, do you not?"

"Oh yes. Oh yes." Philip stood frozen, putty to her advances.

Pandora's fingers danced across his shirt and began to unbutton it. "Then give yourself over to my love."

Philip held statuesque as she yanked his shirt off of his arms.

Pandora's eyes beamed blue in his face. "Release your flood of love, your majesty. For nothing is better than pure love."

The King swooned.

She turned her attention to his pants.

Commotion behind her, the massive oak door wrenched open. Royal troops rushed inside the room with crossbows pointed.

Guided from the rear by that bishop fellow, he screeched out at them, "Seize the witch!"

"Oh no, no no." Pandora shook her head angrily.

More soldiers stumbled into the room to reinforce. Those at the front had frozen with paralysis upon the sight of her nakedness. Others bashed into them from behind.

Crossbows fired. Short arrows impaled Pandora through her belly and chest.

Instantly livid, she roared with Supernatural rage.

"You do not dare!"

An explosion of ultraviolet energy blasted out from her in every direction, sending every human in the room flying back into the stone walls.

"Ahhh!" She pulled out each of the arrows, her face contorted to monstrous proportions. Black vapor escaped from her wounds like a fine mist.

"You ridiculous insects!" Her voice boomed

through the corridors, "You will regret this day."

Pandora dressed herself and strolled forward out of the room, as the remaining humans fled for their lives, abandoning the castle in their chaotic retreat from her.

Strutting down the staircase, she passed the atrium back into the open air. Outside the castle, a final glance at the townsfolk, but they had scattered like rodents from a flood.

Days later she returned and landed in the center of the courtyard again. A similar hysteria erupted immediately. The simpletons trembled in the shadows, hiding themselves from her.

Pandora placed an urn in the courtyard, one with a sealed lid on top. A dirty glance of her glowing green eyes, to the left and to the right, and she shot back up into the sky to disappear from those lands forever.

By the following month, King Philip's entire kingdom lay dead from the Black Plague.

THIRTY SEVEN

The Thornton Building, where Miss Melt occupied the uppermost two floors, poked up beyond the surrounding skyscrapers. It was a major feature of the New York skyline.

Steve Arkin flew through the city labyrinth, spying stealthily from behind the 45th floor of the nearest office tower. He slid silently from spot to spot, as workers inside at their cubicles jumped up, index fingers pointed at him.

The sun held high, and the city sky was a hazy blue.

Steve wondered about the true limitations of his

Supernatural powers, how indestructible he might be given the realities of his encounter with Mr. Stellar. *Just how much force was required to obliterate a Supernatural? Or were they all unique?* These were the big unanswered questions.

Steve knew that Pandora had been truthful when she told him she had D'Andre Walker, and that was unacceptable.

He floated in cautiously toward her line of windows, checked the rooftop, and he continued to scout around the four corners of her silver building, but something seemed off. He had an internal sense about it. A huge reserve of energy lingered nearby. He expected it.

Steve hovered outside of Pandora's portal and he spotted her below in the loft. Inside, she bantered with D'Andre Walker, playing hostess like some sick performance for Steve's benefit.

D'Andre noticed him floating above.

Pandora huffed, and she turned her pink face up to face the window.

Steve heard them through the glass. "Back behind you," said D'Andre.

When he spun to see, the beam hit him full on

from above. Such a blinding flash, concentrated sun pummeling with the force of an earthquake. Thunderous waves exploded down on his head like an inverted volcano.

It was Quakestorm. He commanded the rays of the sun, and it blasted Steve down through the concrete layers below the city. He crashed through subway tunnels in a void of black like some splattered bug.

THIRTY EIGHT

D'Andre struggled up uneasily and stumbled over to Pandora's wall of windows.

"Sorry, kid," said Miss Pandora, behind him. "Arkin's just a big, lovable fool."

D'Andre's hands fell against the plate glass, his palms barely able to steady himself. He had thrown up smoothie all over his shirt, and he felt too weak to stand for too long. He didn't want to fall on the marble, though, because it was so hard.

Far below at the street, Steve had fallen out of view.

Quakestorm, one of the freakiest Supers ever,

held is arms in front of him to make a ball that grabbed the sunlight and focused it down like a big magnifying glass. He dropped past the windows on a beeline after Super Steve, to finish him off.

D'Andre slumped down and slid back against the glass. He had to remember to breathe, or he wasn't going to make it. There wasn't enough oxygen. His body weakened and wouldn't recover. He wished he had an oxygen tank. There wasn't enough air. His head floated in a pounding daze, and his eyes flickered grey. He lay down on the floor, but still there wasn't enough in the air. He watched Miss Pandora's feet move back and forth around her apartment, her glow brightening the loft as she tinkered from flower to flower.

The front door opened up.

Quakestorm carried Super Steve inside over his shoulder.

D'Andre watched helplessly from the floor as the freaky monster deposited Steve's unconscious body in a different room.

Pandora reappeared, bending low with napkins. Her glowing white hand pushed into his face and wiped the mess off.

"You're going to have to keep your food down,

okay? I don't have patience for this."

She lifted D'Andre in the air by his upper arms, held well out in front of her dress, like a doll, and she carried him to the same room where Super Steve had been placed. The smooth cell had a massive steel door, like a bank vault.

Quakestorm wrapped a thick metal chain around Steve, in circle after circle. The chains bound him to a steel supporting column running up through the room.

D'Andre landed in a lumpy heap in the metallic corner of the vault, and he squirmed to right himself.

Breathe or die.

"Could I get some oxygen? Please?" he whispered.

"What?" Pandora shook her head angrily. "It's in the air. We've got to go."

Quakestorm wrapped Steve with so many loops that he stood like a mummy.

The chains jingled, as Steve awakened.

Pandora coaxed the giant stone-faced creature back out. "It's time, Quakey."

Quakestorm yanked on the chains. As he did, energy fields rumbled around him loudly, amplified in that tiny steel vault.

D'Andre lay still in the far corner, his face

flattened into the cold steel floor.

Pandora sashayed out of the doorway. "Quakey, we'll miss it! Dragomir is pretty humorless about this stuff."

Quakestorm turned his rock face, and he stomped ahead to follow her. They sealed and locked the vault door. Thunder gave way to total silence.

It was completely dark. D'Andre groaned with soreness, and he twisted onto his back on the unforgiving metal floor.

Steve woke up. "D'Andre?"

"Huh?"

"Hey. Hey, buddy. Can you move?"

"Uuuugh." D'Andre jolted his head.

"Listen, man," said Steve. "D'Andre? Come on."

D'Andre flopped onto his side to try and locate Steve in the blackness. He couldn't see a thing. It was time to give up, as he had no more oxygen, and his brain wasn't going to make it.

It was okay to die. Everybody died.

THIRTY NINE

High above the New York City skyline, Dragomir hovered to gather his organization into an acceptable flight formation. With a twitch of his wings he reached back and retrieved Woden's silver spear to make use of it.

"It is time we took the reins back."

Nukeman, Barby, Shifty, Quakestorm, and Pandora fell in behind him in the shape of a V.

"I've waited quite long enough for this day."

Dragomir drew back his arm. Gungnir sailed down silently, trailing blue sparkling residue in its wake. The spear blasted a hole into the side of the United Nations building, and Dragomir dove inside to follow it in.

His clique invaded the General Assembly chamber, high above the cowering human diplomats. His spear had lodged itself in the precise center of the marble podium. As his wings flapped widely to affect them all further, he wrenched his spear back from the stone and into his fidgeting claws.

His team dropped inside through that high gash in the outer wall. They hovered at the sides of the stage, beaming out at the humans.

With an utter disregard for the old human protocols, Dragomir stomped to the microphone and began to speak, "A little theatricality goes a long way. Hahahaha. Yes. We are here, and you should listen well, *homo sapiens*."

Pandora and the others floated menacingly on either side of the elevated UN stage. Television cameras recorded the event in full, as Dragomir tapped the mic. His message beamed out live to the human world.

"Good day, people," said the half-dragon.

Diplomats checked their earpieces for translations.

"The title of my speech this day shall be *The New Natural World Order*."

Humans scribbled notes and worked their phones and computers.

Dragomir raised his volume, "Our voices have not received their proper due, in respect to the direction of global events and agreements. How to rectify this shortcoming in the current order? Answer, *we* shall require veto authority over human events."

Murmurs gushed out across the assembly.

"Silence!" He rose up from the platform. "And tribute, precious stones, diamonds, gold, the rarest metals, uranium. You will dig them for us. We shall simply control all major developments on planet earth. This was, of course, *our* planet long before you primitives invented your technologies. It has never ceased being *our planet*."

Dragomir hovered above the others, microphone in his right claw. "And that, my little humans, is the *New Natural World Order*. Thank you very much for your cooperation."

Dragomir dropped the microphone, which echoed with a rumble. Expecting a rousing applause, none came. Instead the diplomats of the human nations gazed on in helpless terror, little caricatures of men, or perhaps more like mice in a snake tank.

Dragomir signaled his crew. His Supernaturals shot up and out through that same hole in the building through which they had entered.

At the UN's gash Miss Melt twisted back, glowing in hot red, and she giggled loudly.

FORTY

Steve's eyes could see moderately well in the darkness of the vault, but he was restrained and immobile. The chains held fast.

D'Andre Walker lay still on the cold steel floor.

Steve rattled the chains and jolted his body to free himself. "Uhhh!" As he flinched and thrashed, the chains seemed to tighten about him.

D'Andre stirred, on the other side of the vault. "You could do it, Steve."

"I can't get any leverage," he said. In the dark something bright glowed radically below him. He looked down.

"D'Andre? Can you see my watch? The numbers are glowing."

"Yeah," said the kid. "I see it now."

"Come here and take it. The watch. It's not a regular watch. Hurry."

D'Andre lifted his head up from the floor. "Aaiight." He crawled so slowly forward.

Time was short. "Come on, buddy. I've got something pretty amazing for you to think about."

D'Andre pulled himself another foot closer. "What?"

"It's a pretty big deal, but you gotta hurry. They're coming back."

D'Andre yanked himself closer another foot. "What is it, Steve?"

Steve hesitated. "Would you be like me?"

The kid stopped crawling from surprise. "What do you? What you mean?"

"Would you become a Supernatural?"

D'Andre tilted his head around in the blackness. "Me? I don't know."

Steve relaxed and sank back into his chains. "Well you better make up your mind fast. Or we might not get another chance."

D'Andre sat up and said, "I could be like you?"

Steve huffed out. "Come over here quick and find out."

D'Andre crawled again toward the watch. He reached and grabbed hold of it.

Steve said, "The clasp on the back."

D'Andre snapped the wristwatch off of Steve's wrist and he fell back to crash on the steel floor. He seemed to be out of energy and his head rolled backward. He closed his eyes again. "Ohh. I don't feel good."

"I know, D'Andre. I know. Can you turn the watch over? The back has to come off."

D'Andre examined the softly glowing timepiece.

"Pop off the back."

"How?"

"Do you have something? A coin?"

"Nah."

"Try your fingernail."

D'Andre couldn't budge it. "It won't go."

"Use your teeth if you have to."

The kid gazed confused. He scraped the steel watch casing with his teeth.

"It won't come."

He tried again.

Finally, the back popped off. Inside, the spy watch contained the little crackling syringe, black but radiating sparks of weird energy.

"Careful. Take it out."

D'Andre looked at it with awe. He had the needle in his hand. "Is it gonna hurt?"

"Yes."

D'Andre paused, unsure.

Steve said, "Try and get it in the vein."

D'Andre straightened up in place. He panted heavily like he was going to pass out. "Just like you?"

"Could be."

The kid stared for the longest time at the crackling sparks orbiting the black liquid inside the syringe.

"Well why not, then? Right?"

Steve's eyes misted over. "You can do it. Nothing stopping you."

D'Andre gazed into the needle.

Steve watched through the darkness, as the kid jabbed his own arm and squeezed the glowing dark matter catalyst into his arteries.

Instantly, D'Andre fell flat on his back, his body

convulsing in violent spasms. A cold dark energy field surrounded him. His skin steamed. He shook wildly on the floor through a transmogrification.

FORTY ONE

In the blackness of the sealed steel vault, D'Andre Walker awakened from his deep coma. His head slowly began to feel again. His eyes brightened, as if someone had turned on all the lights. Soft green glow everywhere. He could see things in the darkness, and he could move again. He looked at his hands, and he jumped up to his feet.

Not just living in normal three-dimensional space, he felt like some kind of conduit between the world and the space of the dark energy. Dark matter fields ebbed and flowed like a gentle tide through his body, from one world to the next and then back. His atoms were energized beyond what any human could experience, except Steve, of course.

D'Andre stood up tall, and he spun around. Then he floated up off the ground.

"Steve! Steve! I'm flyin'."

"Of course," said Super Steve. "See that air vent?" Steve nodded his head up toward the ceiling. He was chained up like a big round ball of metal twine.

"Yeah, I see it." D'Andre floated up to the grate. Up high, the little vault seemed comical. "Hahaha."

Steve said, "Can you fit through there?"

D'Andre's hand grabbed the metal grate covering. He pulled the slotted barrier until the screws popped off.

"Oh my God. I did that?"

"Yes you did," said Steve. "What do you think? Can you get out?"

D'Andre popped his head up into the tiny duct. "Oh I don't know. It's real cramped. And scary in there."

Steve said, "Not as scary as it'll be when they come back here. Hurry."

"Yeah." D'Andre nodded briskly. "Yeah, you right. You right. I could do this."

"You gotta do this, D'Andre."

D'Andre climbed in and contorted his body up into the ventilation duct. It bent and rocked as he wiggled through. He had to turn around at a corner, and then he saw the light stream in at the end of the duct.

His hands pushed out another metal grate, and he found himself in Miss Melt's bedroom, floating around up on the air, curious.

D'Andre turned back to scope out the lay of the suite. "Where's that room at?"

Out of the door and down the hallway. The money vault was sealed up tight. He inspected the big steel door. On one side was a giant handle. He yanked it down. Nothing happened.

"Hmm."

A plate with lit-up numbers seemed inviting. He grabbed it and pulled the steel face off of the security panel.

"Haha!" His hand reached inside, and a number of gears and rods locked the door in place. D'Andre's bare hand grabbed onto a rod, and he ripped it out of the door. The steel piece snapped. He tossed it over his shoulder.

Again he tried the release handle. Nothing.

D'Andre dug both his hands into the guts of the

vault door, and he wrestled out all the rods and gears as fast as he could pull it apart. Fingers dug around in the box until one of the rods slid backward in place, and he heard a loud clank.

When he yanked down on the handle this time another clank popped. The door opened a few inches. Then it stuck in place.

"Oh no you don't!" He flew up sideways with his feet on the wall, and he pulled the edge of the door until it bent and crumpled. The vault popped open completely, and the light streamed in onto Super Steve.

"Did you see that!" D'Andre flew over to Steve's face. "Did you see that?"

"Yeah. I saw it. Can you figure out how this chain is locked please?"

"Yeah, yeah. I got you, Steve. But I mean, I need a picture a that. I mean for serious. You ain't got a camera? Nuthin? Like a camera phone or suttom?"

Steve rattled his head beneath the chains. "Next time."

"Aiight." D'Andre shrugged and flew around behind the building's support column.

"Oh. That little lock! Psssh."

FORTY TWO

Pandora trailed behind Dragomir and his cohorts as they flew over the city back to her building. All of them piled in through her window portal, above her loft. Her impetuous cats raced to hide in the shadows, as the Barbarian squeezed in through the tight opening above.

"Don't break the door," she quipped.

Quakestorm, Nukeman, and a battered Shifty set down behind Dragomir across the loft.

Pandora followed as Dragomir slid Woden's spear from his back, and he clenched his claws tightly onto the blue silver shaft. The spear twinkled with microscopic sparks that left streaks in the air.

As she passed, she grabbed the warm margarita she had hastily left sitting on the bar. Her color scheme adjusted to suit her lightening mood.

Nukeman chattered, "That was a great speech, boss."

Barby nodded. "Mmm. Good words."

"Yes," said Dragomir as he marched through the hallway. "You would assume I'd be feeling a bit more magnanimous. Alas, no." He barked back at Pandora, "Where's Arkin?"

She trotted out ahead in the hallway, streaming peach residue behind her, and she led them all down a half-level and around a corner to the vault. They froze before the dislocated door.

Pandora rushed in. A pile of chains remained, but no one. Her hair chilled to a muted ice blue.

Dragomir filled the vault's doorway in crisp silhouette. "So? Where is the human?"

Quakestorm dropped his gaze.

Pandora pointed her thumb back at Quakey. "Well, he chained him up."

Out in the hallway, the Barbarian's chuckles filled the air.

Dragomir seethed. "I am not sure how I succeed,

when clearly I am drowning in a sea of utter incompetence."

Pandora remained speechless and shrugged.

Dragomir whipped his wings about and stormed past them. He slid his spear once again across his back and disappeared around the corner alone.

Pandora, Quakestorm, Barby, and Nukeman exchanged annoyed glances at one another.

Shifty transformed himself into an egregiously distorted caricature of Dragomir. He wagged a reptilian finger at them all.

The others tried to suppress their mirth, but couldn't.

As Shifty bobbled his dragon head in each of their faces, Pandora roared out, "Hahaha..."

One by one, they jolted and shuffled forward to trail after their leader.

FORTY THREE

'Andre flew to follow Super Steve. It was late afternoon above a forest. He didn't know where he was going. They landed at a wood cabin by a green pond.

D'Andre spun around, taking in the surroundings. "What is this place? This your place? This is nice."

He had never been to a lake before, and this one had its own house.

Into the wooden cabin they strolled.

Steve said, "Are you sure you're all right?"

"I'm better than aiiight!"

D'Andre inspected the living room. It was simple,

bare, but broken wood had landed in the middle of the floor. The sun was streaming in through a hole in the ceiling.

"You get hit by a asteroid or suttom?"

"No,' Steve said, "And I want to tell you don't get overconfident."

"What you mean?"

"I mean we're still up Shadoobee Creek without a paddle."

Steve flopped down onto his old recliner chair. A puff of dust shot up.

D'Andre couldn't decide where to go or what to do. His mind was out of control. With so much energy, he didn't even want to walk if he could fly. His feet floated up, and he circled around the room to inspect the pictures on the walls.

Steve said, "You know that spear that Dragomir always wears?"

"Yeah!" said D'Andre, because he knew all kinds of Supernatural stuff. "Woden's spear. Gungnir."

"There's no defense. It never misses."

"Never?"

"Ever."

Clouds passed. The room flared brightly.

D'Andre looked up at the sun streaming in. Dust and debris had fallen about the mangled hole in the house. "Hey what happened your roof?"

Steve shook his head, annoyed. "I've got to think. Do you understand? They could bust in here any second." Steve closed his eyes and massaged his temples.

D'Andre buzzed around the room quickly like a bee. "So like, what's the plan? We gotta get 'em 'fore they get us. Right?"

"I don't know, kid. Go outside for a swim or something."

D'Andre spied out the cabin's window. "Wow. I ain't been swimmin' in years."

"See. There it is. Have fun. Go talk to the fish."

"Aiight. Talk to the fish! That's pretty good. With no lifeguard?"

Steve rolled his eyes and glanced over.

D'Andre giggled. "Hahahaha..." He pointed up at the ceiling. "You know you should fix your roof, case it rains. My Grandpops could help you out. He's good with tools, building all kinds a stuff. He'll hook you up."

Steve breathed out with exasperation. "Forget the roof. I don't care about the roof right now."

"Naw. I mean later."

"There may not be a later. Let me think, D'Andre."

D'Andre nodded, and he buzzed outside to investigate Super Steve's lake. He flew over the still water taking in the whole secluded valley.

It was like nowhere he'd ever been in his life. There were trees and birds everywhere, and he could see the fish down below the surface. He heard the bird calls and the insects, the bubbles, the wind cutting through the leaves. It was like he could hear everything, and it didn't even look like a regular pond. The colors vibrated like ultraviolet or something.

After he hesitated, D'Andre dove straight down to see about swimming underwater, and talking to them fishes.

FORTY FOUR

Dragomir lifted off from the overcrowded Metropolis, as the electricity surged again below him. The local humans had recovered their energy grid with predicted resilience. The stench of them rose to the upper atmosphere, and he vowed they would clean up their act or be eradicated. If their stink was noticeable by him, of all beings, then they truly infested the planet to the point of saturation. Ecological collapse would soon follow. Maybe it was best for everyone if they all went away.

The age had come again to make examples of them if they were to be brought to heel. Steven Arkin would be the first, the ultimate human example. The message would be that not even a former human would be tolerated within the ranks of Supernaturals. These primates would again know their place in the larger scheme. Arkin had to fall, as he knew too much, particularly the physical location of the *Council of Power*. If he reconciled with the humans and turned their arsenals loose, it represented an unacceptable risk.

Below, on the glacial mountaintop, the bubble in which the fortress masked itself from prying human eyes gleamed momentarily in the morning's glare. Rainbow fringes adjusted in the visual spectrum. The supernatural superstructure sponged up the yellow rays to conceal itself within them.

Dragomir led his generals down and reentered his palace. Trailed by Nukeman and Barby the Barbarian, he ordered that Nukeman hover well above the fortress and keep a watch for Arkin.

The half-dragon sauntered into his presidential suite and he clicked on his wall of television monitors. A dusty old bottle and a box of cigars, a victory glass. Dragomir lit a celebratory smoke. Global news seemed unexceptional, given his revolutionary proclamations.

British state television recapped, "The leaders of

the G-8 nations scrambling to come to some sort of agreement to meet in emergency session. It is unclear if an envoy for the Supernaturals will be present..."

Dragomir smirked. His fingernail flicked on a video-conference screen.

"Inform the G-8 that I'd very much like to sit in, as just a quiet observer. No bother at all."

He stretched back in his tall office chair, and he flopped his feet up onto the desk, puffing his cigar alone in the barricaded rock fortress. Patiently, he awaited the next human development to flash across his many screens.

FORTY FIVE

Steve flew across the globe, avoiding dark matter signatures below, which churned in his guts and guided his course wide of them. Above the snowy white mountain range, he set down in a Pakistani parking lot where rows of beat-up 18-wheel tractor-trailers rotted. He lifted the front end of one and snatched the disabled truck by its front axle. Off the ground, he hauled it up toward higher elevations.

Blankets of puffy fog as far as he could see, his shadow slithered from peak to slope and undulated over the white ridges through the wisps of moisture. Steve forged ahead on a direct line, dragging the tractor trailer in one hand.

He knew there was a time when icy steel would have frozen his skin and killed it with frostbite. His mind recalled his young son Michael and their first snowball fight in the backyard. Cathy and the boy rushed outside to experience the first snowfall of the year. Unprepared for the stinging coldness they grabbed at the snow and threw snowballs at one another. The fight escalated, despite the pain of bare skin on ice. As long as Cathy tossed snowballs back at him, he persisted. She was wild and let loose. He loved to see her so excited. Eventually, their hands reddened and their nerves screamed. With their fists clenched up uselessly, he and Cathy gave up on the snowball battle.

Michael was three or four, and he was the first to quit. They noticed him crying behind them in the snow. Steve pulled him up and rushed him inside the house to run warm water over his tiny red hands.

"Sorry, Mikey. You gotta remember gloves next time."

"I don't like it!" he cried.

That was all Steve could remember of the incident, that and Cathy's quirky smile burned forever in him, which he now missed every day. When he shook his head, snow fell out all over the kitchen like dandruff. That amused Cathy, and she tossed his hair around with her fingertips.

As Steve flew on to face the *Council of Power* alone, like a guided missile, lugging the old truck, he could feel dark energy imbalances popping around him in the atmosphere. Heightened activity splashed from that unknowable dimension. They closed in, but they kept hidden across the landscape and the atmosphere. Regardless, Steve plunged ahead, dragging that old rusty truck over the mountains with purpose.

Above the *Council* fortress the upper regions of the stratosphere soon populated with a growing audience. Supernaturals lingered overhead to rubberneck. They all seemed to know something was in process.

In the *Council* fortress below, the courtyard remained empty.

Steve closed in those several remaining miles.

"Dragomir!"

Supernaturals appeared from within the entrance passageway. News traveled inside. Dark energy fields sizzled and roared. More creatures arrived to witness.

"Dragomir!" yelled Steve Arkin. "Get out here!"

Barby the Barbarian and Mr. Nukeman rocketed upward, followed instantly by Dragomir himself. Already, he held Woden's spear at the ready. The three of them zipped up several hundred feet to confront Steve.

Supernatural beings poured out of the fortress to watch Steve hover above the mountain slope. Spectators raced in above and took positions across the puffy grey sky, the haze littered with wrinkles and twinkles of unknown origin.

Dragomir comported himself below the crowd, leading his clique higher to directly face Steve. Flapping his wings sharply, he settled at a distance and hovered still, surprised by the thickening audience of Supernaturals.

Supers watched from high above, below, and all around them.

Nukeman spoke, "Boss—"

"Leave him for me." Dragomir flicked his wings and sailed out in front of them all.

Steve dragged his trailer truck in closer, his eyes

fixed on Dragomir.

His adversary cautiously sized up the tractor-trailer.

Remaining Supers piled out of the *Council* fortress, and they took to the air, which was thick with throbbing dark energy, swirling around their standoff. The cloudy sky had filled with most of the earth's Supernaturals, hundreds, many invisible, and without even an invitation.

Steve took a long moment to assess the half-dragon. Woden's silver spear gleamed blue in Dragomir's claws.

Dragomir sneered back. "If only I knew it was this easy to summon you, Arkin."

The half-dragon again assessed the expanding dark-energy audience, which closed in tighter to better witness.

Steve called back, "You told the world I like to throw vehicles around. So let's party."

Dragomir laughed heartily. "Hahaha... You're trying to distract me with silliness." He checked behind him. Nukeman and Barby spun likewise with paranoia.

Steve addressed the Supernatural crowd, "If not for that stolen spear, why would anyone want to follow you?"

The cordon of Supernaturals squeezed in closer from their various points on the compass. The clouds above dimmed from the weight of their presence.

Dragomir waved casually. "Because I'm right." He launched the spear at Mach 10 directly at Steve's abdomen.

Steve released the truck and clasped both his hands onto the hypersonic projectile. The tip of it penetrated his skin for half an inch, and then erupted in a storm of dancing bolts of energy. The spear's power enveloped Steve's entire body in its bubble.

The trailer truck bounced harmlessly down the snowy slope, as Steve Arkin yanked the spear's tip out from his skin, and he turned it around.

Another massive jolt encapsulated Steve, as he absorbed the blue lightning charges.

He held up Gungnir in his left hand to show them all. "Thanks, buddy."

Dragomir's face drooped, and he paled with horror.

Nukeman and Barby stared blankly in disbelief.

Murmurs shot across the sky.

Steve examined the ancient weapon. It seemed

alive, reactive to his touch.

Dragomir and his co-conspirators fled for their lives. Instantly they ducked behind the mountain range on a frenetic retreat across the continent.

The Supernatural onlookers arrived above the *Council* fortress, and they stared silently back at Steve Arkin.

They all seemed so foreign and so cryptic. He rotated in a slow circle, spear in hand, all eyes on him. Taking in their responses, he felt surrounded. So many Supers, which he had never before seen, let alone communicated with. They came from under the oceans, beneath the lands, from orbit, and from the remotest locales hidden from human encroachment. They kept a distance from him and seemed apprehensive.

Steve lowered the spear to his side, and he dropped down into the *Council* fortress.

"Come on. Gather all Supernaturals."

The great mass of earth's Supers flowed into the *Council of Power* behind him.

Into Dragomir's presidential office Steve stepped alone. There he found the old dusty lever to activate that ancient clarion call. He glanced around at the numerous screens.

Pandora glowed brightly on one, no-doubt lying to all of humanity again. That was her job.

The bell rumbled the earth again and again.

Steve marched out into the stone corridor alone. Once inside the *Great Hall*, the full population of Supers arrived. No more could fit in the cavern. Even the lobby was packed with never-before-witnessed life-energy forms.

He gazed out, as it was truly a gathering to remember. Steve's feet ascended the old stone staircase to the stage platform, and he looked out across them all.

The clarion bell ceased.

Before him were such exotic creatures who waited patiently, vibrating in their own ways. Many looked so old as to be immobile and sickly. Others appeared alien. All of their eyes fixed up on him. He wasn't sure what to make of them.

Steve discovered D'Andre Walker in a seat in the center of the *Great Hall*. His wide eyes gawked around the room, and he jolted repeatedly as he noticed the ancients.

All stared up at Steve at the center podium. They may have been more concerned about the spear in his hand. That was the first thing he needed to address.

He stepped to the microphone, and it amplified his voice above the din of the hall. "Please. I would like to say two things, if I may."

The *Great Hall* quieted to solemnity, unlike any silence found in human civilization. All the air's vibrations ceased, arrested, muffled by the pressing of dark matter within that sealed, solid-rock temple.

Steve announced to them, "For murdering, in cold blood, President Woden as well as a number of innocent human beings, it is my opinion that Dragomir and his accomplices have worn out their welcomes on planet earth, and they should go and find a different planet to dwell on."

Whispers fanned across the gathered Supernatural crowd. Energy fields rumbled. Scrapes and hisses swelled toward a crescendo.

Steve didn't know what it meant, and he paused for their dark cacophony to silence again.

"They should be banished from our beautiful home world. That is our responsibility here today."

Earth's Supernatural legions discussed among themselves in hushed confusing streams of energy.

He nodded.

"All who agree," Steve said forcefully, "raise your

hands, or say aye to be counted. Please."

None of the Supers moved. The entire *Great Hall* lingered in still trepidation.

"Aye!" yelled D'Andre Walker.

Those gathered turned to assess the boy, who stood with his arm held high.

Others raised their hands.

Suddenly, a wave rippled over the Supernatural crowd until there was unanimous agreement. "Aye, aye, aye, aye…"

Steve nodded with relief.

"We will all make it happen." In his right hand, he lifted Woden's unstoppable spear above his head.

The crowd leaned subtly back in their pews, transfixed by the potential of the legendary weapon. The room quieted again.

Steve floated up above them with the spear in hand.

"The second thing I want to say is that I do not seek power, and I do not want this object."

At rocket speed Steve shot over them all and back out of the *Great Hall,* through the foyer, out to the courtyard and past the statue of Icarus wearing eagle's wings.

He blasted up toward space, leaving them all behind far below.

Assorted Supernaturals piled out of the *Council* fortress after him, and some pursued to watch, keeping their safe distances.

When Steve reached the upper stratosphere, where the blue sky met the blackness and the stars, he slowed. With Gungnir firmly in his grip, he slid on a pair of sunglasses, which reflected the white-hot solar rays raining radiation directly on him.

Confident in his weightless orbit, he held above the world and examined the spear and its outpouring of blue sparks. He considered the situation for a final moment before acting. Below him, he felt the great dark mass shift and the gravitational field skew from those Supernaturals rising up toward him.

With all his strength, Steve heaved the unrestrainable weapon directly at the sun. It soon disappeared on a long journey to the center of a burning star.

D'Andre Walker ascended to see, trailed by dozens of other Supers. Only D'Andre approached Steve.

Steve smiled, and he turned back to face the blue ball of earth.

"Never misses."

D'Andre looked off for the spear, squinting in the harsh glare. He turned his head away to check back down on the world.

"Steve. We're in outer space."

"Yeah."

D'Andre shrugged. "I guess I'd like to take that flight now."

Steve relaxed.

They floated for a few moments in the still embrace of the vacuum.

"Take your time. Take it all in. It's a hell of a planet."

Far below them, the cadre of Supernaturals dispersed across the sky. Little shooting stars streaked in various directions like radioactive particles. He felt their motions more than he could see them.

Steve offered his hand, and D'Andre shook it. They shared a final second in low orbit. Then D'Andre Walker zoomed off back down and across the ocean.

Steve watched D'Andre fly off and descend into the haze of clouds. He too descended and rifled back in an entirely different direction.

FORTY SIX

Pandora, Dragomir, Barby the Barbarian, Nukeman, Quakestorm, and Shifty were soon surrounded by a posse of a hundred Supernaturals.

Steve and D'Andre Walker joined in their encirclement. The world's greatest assemblage of power ever known forced the guilty upward and out like a living net.

Pandora and the other guilty parties found themselves pushed from the planet's comforting atmosphere as the cordon tightened around them. Ejected from earth, they fled toward the black. Earth receded far below.

Pandora's tear froze instantly to her glowing cheek. She flicked it off with her index finger. Head turned to glare at Dragomir, her green radiating eyes filled with frustrated rage. Her voice crackled in the radio spectrum like chips of ice. "This was all your plan!"

"Oh, shut it!"

The rogues searched across the galaxy, unsure and afraid. Their physical bodies soon petrified and took on statuesque textures.

Dragomir surged ahead of the pack, attempting to lead them toward some random new star.

Pandora saw Barby wipe his own frozen tears off of his cheek.

Their gang took in a final glimpse of the tiny blue sphere behind them, and the vanquished Supernaturals receded into a vast black abyss.

FORTY SEVEN

Supernatural D'Andre Walker figured out which direction was which, and he flew alone back up to New York City. Over the Bronx, he navigated his way above the street grid to Queens borough. Eventually, he settled on his Grandpops' house, and he descended back to earth.

It was early morning, a crisp hazy workday in the big city. Grandpops' old beat up Ford was running in the driveway. Then Grandpop slammed his front door shut and locked it on his way to work.

D'Andre hid himself behind a parked car on the street. With a devilish smile he watched Grandpops. When the old man climbed into his driver's seat,

D'Andre flew over low and lifted up the front of the vehicle, where the engine was, high up over his head.

"What the hell!" Grandpops yelled all over the street. "Oh my! What the hell!"

Grandpops jerked the steering wheel and honked the horn loud in a frenzy. "Oh Jesus! No!"

D'Andre lowered the truck back down and laughed raucously. He floated up in front of the windshield.

"It's me!"

Grandpop's jaw hung open, and he jolted his head. "What are you doin?"

"I'm flyin'."

"Well I could see that, boy. How you doin' it?"

"Supernatural stuff." D'Andre giggled, as his Grandpops shook his head in disbelief, his hand over his mouth.

"Oh Lord," said the old man. "Never thought I'd see this day."

D'Andre set down beside the driver's side door, where he laughed to himself.

Grandpops shut off his engine and climbed out of the truck. "Well, you shouldn't go pickin' up people's trucks like that, boy. What's the matter with you?

Nearly gave me a heart condition. It's still beatin' all crazified. So, let me get a good look at ya."

Grandpops bent down low, and his giant hand squeezed D'Andre's shoulder. "All right. You look pretty much the same. So how'd all this happen?"

They headed inside the house.

As he remembered stuff, D'Andre rambled through many details from the past week in a crazy stream of consciousness that he knew probably didn't make that much sense.

Grandpops fixed him a peanut butter and jelly sandwich, nodding his head a lot. Grandpops seemed to play it cool. He just nodded, and said, "Mmmhmmm."

D'Andre finally ran out of story to tell, and he shrugged. "So what do you think I should do now?"

"Well," Grahdpops took in a slow deep breath, and he sipped his cup of coffee. "That's a super-sized question, grandson. Let me think on it a while. You absolutely sure you all better now? The sickness left ya?"

"I feels great!"

"Now, that is the best news I heard in years. Believe you me. Thank God for that. Thank God you all right now. It's overwhelmin', is what it is. I just need a minute to think straight about all this Supernatural business."

"You want me to do suttom Supernatural, Grandpops?"

The old man held up his palm. "Now hold on a second, boy. Let's think about this. That's a serious proposition, a weighty, heavy proposition. You understand me? Not to be taken lightly. You gonna have to grow up fast now."

D'Andre sat back down and munched on his PB&J sandwich.

Grandpops eyes glanced over slyly, "There is somethin' I gots for ya."

D'Andre sprng up tall in his chair. "Yeah? Let's do it!"

"Now hold on, now. Hold yourself. It's not what you're thinkin'. It's not gonna be easy."

"So, what?" D'Andre waited for a new idea, a new project.

"I do want you to do somethin' for me, D'Andre. Somethin' for everybody. Understand?"

"Aiight. I'm down." D'Andre felt so much energy bursting out in every direction, there was nothing scaring him now. He stared up quizzically.

"I want you—listen carefully now." Grandpops had a tendency to over-dramatize things and be annoying.

"I'm listenin' Grandpops. Come on!" His arms shook with tension, as the old man slowly settled into his chair beside him.

"Mmmhmm... I want you to get a education. A *real* education. Find out what the hell is goin' on out there. World's full a liars, deceivers. Professionals. They on every channel. Nobody knows what's what no more. It's confusion, mass confusion, delusion, all kinds a crazy nowadays."

D'Andre frowned. "School?"

"Yeah, school. D'Andre. But more than that. Listen up. Real learnin'. Not just sit there and do what they tell ya. Challenge what they say. Go further. Find out for yo self. Find out as much information as you can before you act on somethin' and destroy somethin' people built over generations of hard work. There's a reason they built that stuff in the first place. What's that reason? You gotta solve problems, not make more of 'em."

D'Andre nodded.

Grandpops stared back stoically, like a rock. "You

feel me? The world's a mighty big place, and things ain't always obvious why they're this way or that. You need to educate yourself. Find out why. That's what I want you to do, little man. Be super smart. Not just super strong."

D'Andre sat, frustrated.

Grandpops pointed at his own head. "Strength without knowledge is weakness. You put your strength into the opposite direction of where it needs to go. That's called counterproductive. Don't be counterproductive. You gotta lead in the forward direction. Then you can make things better for everybody."

D'Andre silently nodded back.

"It's an incredible gift you got with ya now, D'Andre. It's fantastic. And you gotta own it right from the start. You could make some big things happen, but you could make big mistakes too. Right?"

D'Andre nodded.

"Lord knows I made so many over my lifetime. Wish I could take 'em back too. But you can't. It's better not to make 'em in the first place."

D'Andre broke from his meditative lull, and he peered up into his Grandpop's face.

"I got you, Grandpops. I got you."

\#

Follow the Author

Twitter
@joegiambrone

Blog
https://jgiambrone.wordpress.com/

Goodreads
https://www.goodreads.com/author/show/8506043.J_
Giambrone

Reviews are always welcome.

Thank you!

Books by
J. Giambrone

**Hell of a Deal:
A Supernatural Satire**
2010

Transfixion
2014

Wrecking Balls
2017

Demigods
2019